Lisa Jenkins

'Sexy'
Louise Mullins

'Suspenseful'
A. J. Thomas

DARK EDGE PRESS

THE WIDOW

IVAN JENSON

Published in 2022 by Dark Edge Press.

Y Bwthyn
Caerleon road,
Newport,
Wales.

www.darkedgepress.co.uk

Text copyright © 2022 Ivan Jenson

Cover Design: Jamie Curtis

Cover Photography: Canva

The moral right of Ivan Jenson to be identified as the author of this work has been asserted in accordance with the Copyright, Designs and Patents Act 1988.

All rights reserved, including the right to reproduce this book, or portions thereof in any form. No part of this text may be reproduced, transmitted, downloaded, decompiled, reverse engineered, stored, or introduced into any information storage and retrieval system by any means, whether electronic or mechanical without the express written permission of the author.

This is a work of fiction. Names, characters, places, incidents and dialogues are products of the author's imagination or are used fictitiously. Any resemblance to actual people, living or dead, events or locales is entirely coincidental.

A CIP catalogue record for this book is available from the British Library.

ISBN (eBook): B09H4PNHMT
ISBN (Paperback): 979-8-4214-0088-2

CONTENTS

CHAPTER ONE

CHAPTER TWO

CHAPTER THREE

CHAPTER FOUR

CHAPTER FIVE

CHAPTER SIX

CHAPTER SEVEN

CHAPTER EIGHT

CHAPTER NINE

CHAPTER TEN

CHAPTER ELEVEN

CHAPTER TWELVE

CHAPTER THIRTEEN

CHAPTER FOURTEEN

CHAPTER FIFTEEN

CHAPTER SIXTEEN

CHAPTER SEVENTEEN

CHAPTER EIGHTEEN

CHAPTER NINETEEN

CHAPTER TWENTY

CHAPTER TWENTY-ONE

CHAPTER TWENTY-TWO

CHAPTER TWENTY-THREE

CHAPTER TWENTY-FOUR

CHAPTER TWENTY-FIVE

CHAPTER TWENTY-SIX

CHAPTER TWENTY-EIGHT

CHAPTER TWENTY-NINE

CHAPTER THIRTY

CHAPTER THIRTY-ONE

CHAPTER THIRTY-TWO

CHAPTER THIRTY-THREE

CHAPTER THIRTY-FOUR

CHAPTER THIRTY-FIVE

CHAPTER THIRTY-SIX

CHAPTER THIRTY-SEVEN

CHAPTER THIRTY-EIGHT

CHAPTER THIRTY-NINE

CHAPTER FORTY

CHAPTER FORTY-ONE

CHAPTER FORTY-TWO

CHAPTER FORTY-THREE

CHAPTER FORTY-FOUR

CHAPTER FORTY-FIVE

CHAPTER FORTY-SIX

CHAPTER FORTY-SEVEN

CHAPTER FORTY-EIGHT

CHAPTER FORTY-NINE

CHAPTER FIFTY

CHAPTER FIFTY-ONE

CHAPTER FIFTY-TWO

CHAPTER ONE

SYLIVA

I lost my second husband, the love of my life, to a murder-suicide attempt that wound up only killing one of us. Yes, he loved me that much that he would rather see me dead than with another man. Unfortunately, he was dealing with me, and I would be damned if I would let a man with a deadly obsession drag me down to his level, and in this case that level was death itself. I was twenty-nine years old at the time – it was a year ago today.

His biggest mistake was thinking he could do me in with his bare hands. And while making love no less. He was just rising up from between my legs, his lips glistening, brown eyes wide. He began to kiss my breasts then stopped, which was not part of the script.

I had been enamored by Will. He was one of those thirty-five-year-old guys with long Jesus Christ, light brown hair and a slight beard he never really grew into. Women loved him for his tortured, intellectual charms and I was not immune to his analysis of literary works and his critique of modern culture and his hatred of social media. That's right, he was not a scroller. When I met him he only had a landline phone and I found it to be alarming at first. Imagine having a boyfriend that you could not call at the drop of a dime. Imagine if you were jonesing for some Pringles and had no way of reaching your boyfriend at the grocery store.

So back to that morning.

I was still trembling from the feel of his tongue on my clit when he put his hands round my throat. And then as his grip tightened.

I kept thinking this was some sort of fetish. So at first I didn't fight back. But when the pain started and my windpipe closed, that changed the whole scenario. I began to gag. And I grabbed his wrist, managing to just gurgle the words, "Please, no!"

A knee to my beloved husband's groin changed the power dynamic. And a second knee to the same ultra sensitive part of the man I loved body and soul and he went pale, limp and let go. I then pushed him off of me. Trying to regain his composure he rolled off the bed and so did I. I still somewhat thought this was all part of some kinky role play he'd forgotten to ask my consent for.

Then he stood crouched and wobbled towards me with a fury I had only had glimpses of before, when he would act possessive of me at parties when I was talking to other men. Now, it was all flashing before me. How he would never allow me to have facial recognition on my phone because he felt he had the right to check on who was in contact with me. However, considering he was a terribly sexy professor of English lit at the local community college, I always looked the other way. Now the red flags were all coming together all at once.

Then as Will came at me with that same crazed look in his eyes I stepped aside and ran from the room down the stairs and to the kitchen. He came after me. Talk about the war of the sexes. I could not imagine what had come over him. I was now living within my own personal horror flick. I stood in the kitchen hunting for my smart phone in its glittery pink case. For some reason I didn't even want to flee unless I held it in my hands. I was lost without it. I saw it next to my French press coffee maker, beside the cup of cold coffee I had been enjoying just before my husband had seduced me into a bit of late morning delight which had turned out to be the prelude to my murder.

When my husband stepped into the kitchen he had upped the ante as he now held a pistol in his hand. We had never allowed a gun in our house and so seeing it was literally like seeing an elephant in the room. When did he get it? This was a man who often raised his voice. Yet I always let it slide. He was just the hot-tempered type. And I was okay with it. He was the bitter academic whose novels had never been finished much less published. They were all manifestos to some ballet dancer he had passionately loved on the Upper West side of Manhattan. He mentioned her often. How she had left him standing on Columbus avenue, waiting for hours. She stood him up on the fourth of July back in 2000. And he never found out where she went. And it fucking haunted him for a decade. *What an angry beast of a soul!* I thought to myself whenever he told me about his little tragedy. *Get over it!* I had been stood up many times by bad boys and a few butch femmes. What the hell! My motto has always been that when stood up one should just get thee to a bar, get plastered and fuck someone else.

He shot the first bullet. It struck my shoulder – the one with the tattoo of my first husband's name, Joe, on it. A jerk who left me with a broken heart. Perhaps there is a part of me that I lost when he left me for an older woman. A sugar momma who was willing to finance his post-grunge doodling on his Fender Stratocaster. More power to him. Though as far as I know he has yet to become a post-grunge star. Somebody needs to tell him rock and roll died after Nirvana. Yet the two of them have a child of their own. While my life has become tangled with lovers and leavers ever since I first made love – at the age of sixteen – to a guy who took me to the junior prom and gave me a hit of acid that made us talk to each other about just about everything until the sun rose on my freshly lost virginity. It has been a string of lovers ever since then, alternating between shy introverts and brash obnoxious extroverts. Or to put it simply: good boys and bad boys. And a few girls in between.

After he shot me in the shoulder, Will, my late husband, lost hold of his gun out of a bad case of the jitters. We both looked at it, where it had fallen on the kitchen floor mat and then at each other.

And then I leapt for it, took hold of the gun and stark naked and kneeling, aimed it up at my love.

The veins were bulging on his forehead.

"Step back."

I was still on hands and knees holding the gun, my shoulder bleeding out, and Will was standing there hairy and naked like some above-average looking guy in a gym locker room.

I never thought the day would come that I would aim a gun at my husband. We had only been married for a mere eight months. There were good times. When his mood was stable. And bad times, when he would go ballistic over some petty jealousy over me. I should have left him before. But I loved him for his academic mind, which unfortunately came with a volcanic temper.

"You won't go through with it," he said.

"Were you going to go through with it?"

With an amused look on his face he inched towards me.

"I said step back!"

And then it happened. I had not planned on it. In fact I wasn't sure what I was going to do. I wasn't the one with a plan like he had. No, I was not capable of killing my husband. But the trigger went off as if of its own accord. As if another force that was protecting me, had pulled it. The sound deafened me for a moment. And then when my hearing resumed he was on the floor gripping his stomach.

He turned towards me and reached out for my ankle, squeezing it.

And then once again the trigger seemed to go off by itself, this time shooting him in the chest. The force of the bullet pushed him against the kitchen cabinets. He gasped and then exhaled for the last time. His body growing limp.

I was now looking at the dark side of love, stripped of all boundaries. All abnormalities of our marriage had come to their sudden crystallization. His head flopped over, his neck muscles no longer able to hold it upright.

Will was dead. Yet I was still alive. And thus began an era of my life that was tainted in blood.

CHAPTER TWO

WILL

I watch her now. Knowing more than she would admit. Today she rises at around 7 a.m. worrying more about her golden retriever named Sweetie than she ever did about me.

The dog has a stomach upset and Sylvia is trying to coax her into eating. The truth is Sweetie will soon be here. Where I am. Fourteen years old is ancient for a dog. I will take care of her when she arrives. That is if Sylvia is willing to let go of what she calls her "baby" since we never had one of our own.

Oh, Sylvia! I wish my lips could touch your lips now. And not necessarily the ones on your face. Why did things change between us so much? The last time we made love was the exception to the rule. The rare favor that you had been granting me less and less. You were drifting from me. There was a time when we made love constantly and everywhere. And in the afterglow we would sleep and then eat junk food and watch Netflix. Fucking, eating and Netflix. That was our life. And to think it all started at a small wintry cocktail party, where we were the only two singles. Everyone else was coupled up. We started talking and hit it off right away. We were drinking hot spiked cider and talking. We moved away from the others and wound up in the room with the bed that had all the winter coats piled on top of it and that was where we smoked a joint and drank directly from a bottle of champagne I had snatched from the hostess's fridge. Everyone at the party was on some sort of powder that the hostess had passed around on a plate. Probably good old fashioned Quaaludes. The party had become more like a cult gathering of worshipers of the Spirit of good ole Dave Mathews tunes.

The snow storm was heavy that night. And we were all snowed in. Trashed and wasted. So we crawled under the faux fur coats and the down, suede and leather jackets and you slipped off your panties and said, "I can't believe I am doing this. Well, happy New Year, whoever you are."

And I said, "Whoever you are, I want to be with you till the end of time."

"How poetic," you countered, sticking your tongue down my throat. Then you burped from the champagne bubbles and giggled.

"Of course I'm poetic, I teach English lit," I said.

And then you said, "Suck on my American clit."

And now look at you. Leading the life of a single soon-to-be-thirty woman. I left you behind. You fucked it all up. We were both supposed to be where I am now. How could I drop the fucking gun? What a fumbling fool!

I torture myself as I watch you with your new guy. You didn't wait long. What was it, only four months later that you took up with the chiseled guy that cleared the gutters of what was once our little two-story house on Wealthy Street in East Town? I was right all along. You have always been more than capable of loving another. Of course, he accepted your offer of a cup of java. He took it with sugar and cream. Loads and loads of sugar.

I can read your mind now and I know all about how you found his five o'clock shadowed, Marlboro cowboy look appealing. A man with dirty and callused hands. Filthy finger nails. A manual labor kind of dude, unlike me. I once had smooth palms because I never did much more than rake and mow the lawn. Mostly, I was a man of letters and papers to grade and yes for a time I had an affair with one of my coeds. You don't know about any of that. And you never have to know. You see even a man who is obsessed with utterly possessing his beautiful brunette wife could have some secrets of his own.

I admit that a certain student named Emma went out with me for mugs of beers in the fall, both of us wearing thick sweaters and scarves. Together she and I sipped dark ale at the trendy little place called Harmony in East Town, dangerously close to home. She also loved Thomas Mann, and Nabokov. She said she wanted to write her thesis on "love" and that she needed to research what it was actually like and I took the bait and asked her how it could be that such a buxom twenty-one-year-old English major, with sexy, thick-rimmed glasses could never have experienced love. And she said she didn't want to go into that. She claimed to be a bookish introvert and that she had only just bloomed that fall, that Thursday night, and at that very moment over beers.

We fucked in my car while listening to The Smiths. Morrissey's melancholy voice lilting over our moans. The car windows fogging up. The guilt bubbling up inside me like the spirits of the beer I'd drunk. And yes, I was to see her for the full fall semester term until she cut it off because she had met the man she was going to marry.

I saw them both in the halls of Grand Valley State

University. He had a long Modigliani face and a protruding Adam's apple like an honest young Abe Lincoln. But he was tall. So very tall. He was like some kind of kid giant. He towered and casted a shadow over her. No wonder she said he made her feel "protected" and she didn't want to lose him. She also said she told him all about me because they had vowed to a love of complete honesty and transparency. And I took that as a dire warning that word could get out and I could lose my pending tenure. So I acted as though I never knew her at all. Yet, something about taking up with her. With having that sordid campus affair got me thinking that if I was capable of such deception then Sylvia was too. And so I kept a close eye on my wife. I began to detect a crack in the perfect vase that held the flowers of our love.

You see it takes one to know one.

And now there you are, Sylvia, with your roofer, going out to dinners at the Outback, eating rare steaks and blooming onion rings. There you are on another night sitting at a sushi bar laughing over saki and salmon roe with quail eggs. Looks like you found a real strapping man with a six pack.

He is indeed ripped and lithe and only two years younger than you. He runs his own business and he loves his mom.

Then comes the heartbreaking night when you discover he is a felon and has spent time in jail for car-jacking and breaking into a popular local eatery by throwing a brick into the window. And of course that was all when he was just seventeen years old. Yet he can never shake off his record. You reluctantly accepted him whole-heartedly and unequivocally because he is your type.

The former bad boy.

There has to be a way I can bring you here.

With me.
With us.
The dead.

CHAPTER THREE

ANNE

I am tossing and turning in bed. I just can't sleep. I get up and walk zombie-like, like a Halloween ghoul around the darkened house, mumbling to myself. I feel like a walking, talking ghost that nobody can see.

My husband is fast asleep and snoring.

I am up and around because I am worried about Sylvia. I just want to see her happy. After that traumatic incident that happened to her I imagine she is just putting on a front when she smiles and laughs and acts as chipper as she always has, ever since she was a little girl.

I know my daughter too well. She was our only child. I hardly nursed her though a full term because I simply ran out of milk. They say that does things to a child. At first I followed a book by Doctor Spock and then gave up and just let her be. Let her bounce off the walls. Gave her unbounded freedom. And she was the happiest child. And she was a happy young adult until the unthinkable happened.

I know the likelihood of her being a victim once again are a million to one. And that chance of her having to save herself like she did so bravely that day are also a million to one.

To keep myself busy I sit at the sewing machine. Sylvia has always said she wanted a dress with a Spanish flourish. I think of my own mother who is gone. How she taught me to sew. I have yet to turn on the sewing machine. I am content in my procrastination.

I have lived through the sixties, seventies, eighties and nineties. And I have always been a strong woman. Really, I am just a mother who forever watches over her daughter.

I am not really here. My husband is a widow and I just haunt this house. And no, the dress will never be made and my daughter will never wear it because it is made of quantum energy, from a place that I hope my daughter does not see for many years. Not before she finds true love. Not before she finds redemption. Not before she has a child of her own.

What I am saying is that although I am not of the world any more I still want happiness for my living daughter.

I know she misses me. Oh how she sat at my deathbed and cried and held my hand for that last week of my life. She sobbed like it was a scene from an Italian opera. My sweet baby girl.

My husband, Harold, just got up and is already making himself a breakfast of scrambled eggs, English muffin and coffee with a splash of whole milk. He is utterly alone. He lost me. I lost him. I don't expect him to find another love at fifty-eight. But who knows? The main problem is that he doesn't even try. He just goes about his day, his errands and he doesn't think of love. I wish I could get him to go on a dating app for silver singles. But there is no way for me to reach him now. I can only watch. Watch as, after cleaning up his breakfast dishes, he showers his stocky body and washes it with Old Spice soap, humming a song by James Taylor. Something about the secret of life being enjoying the passage of time.

My dear living husband, I wish you could see me standing in your room. I am the woman that you loved deeply although we fought like Pit Bulls in an illegal dog fight. Right in front of Sylvia. Always about money or some random man you saw me interacting with. The postman, the carpet cleaner, the plumber. Why did I smile like that? How could I touch his arm? It's no wonder Sylvia ended up choosing a possessive man just like you. It was so predictable that she would choose a college professor like her father. Yet you would never strike a woman. Will, on the other hand, tried to kill our daughter.

I knew the guy was messed up from the first time I met that maniac. I knew that he was wrong for her. It all happened too damn fast between them both. I never had any problem with people jumping right into relationships. In my daughter's case she was won over by their talks of DH Lawrence and his midnight recitations of Dylan Thomas and whispered words of TS Eliot.

It was a literate love affair from the start.

My husband was an ace tennis player and a black belt in Karate. He would have ripped Will limb from limb and then jabbed his hand into his throat and cut off his air passage if he had been there to protect Sylvia the morning that it happened.

Harold gets in the car. It is fall, there is a chill in the air. He starts the car. He is about to see the apple of his eyes. He is a shell of a man. Without me that is. But he still has her.

CHAPTER FOUR

SYLVIA

Dad meets me at the indie book store on 28th street that serves up a grand brunch. He is dressed in loose Gap kaki slacks, a gorgeous oversized sweater that shows that still, at fifty-eight, he has biceps to make the elder ladies swoon. We embrace, and as usual he smells of Old Spice and far too much conditioner for his thick head of brunette hair with only a few streaks of grey. My father is devilishly handsome. So much so that the curvy, plus-sized, sexy girl behind the counter with stark green hair smiles at him while asking, "And what can I get for *you*, sir." She really put an emphasis on "*you*." She almost sang it. He could find a new wife in no time at all. If he would only get out and about more.

"I will have a half turkey sandwich and soup. The three bean chili soup sounds delish," he says to the barista.

"It is delish. You will love it. I always have it on my lunch break. Good choice. And what do *you* want?" She says, "*you*" with great despondency. She surely thinks I am his date. They all do. When you have a dad who looks like the father in a daytime soap, what do you expect?

My mom and dad were a gorgeous couple who eloped in their late teens and had me right away. I grew up in like a minute and I always felt more like their roommate. It was a hip environment to come of age. I really miss my mom. She died too young. It's not fair. She was a vegan and she made all sorts of vitamin-infused fruit and vegetable smoothies and still it came for her – the cancer, of the spine. All at once. I remember how she felt so much pain that she would not be able to sleep. She always had trouble sleeping but this was something much worse. And we kept taking her to the doctor and for futile physical therapy. What a joke that was! And then they gave her a CT scan and just as the doctor was about to give her the bad news she interrupted him by saying, "I know by the look in your eyes what it is, Doc, you don't have to tell me."

"Mrs. Henderson, we don't do pain here. You won't have any more pain. We will make sure of that," he said.

I don't want to think about it now. I want to enjoy the one parent that I have here with me now. I sit across from my dad, basking in the glow of his full attention.

"So, how are you doing with your new squeeze?" he asks.

"We are doing alright. You know damn well I am going easy on all that stuff. No more rushing into things. I have learned my lesson."

"I don't blame you."

We aren't even exclusive. I can't be boxed in any more."

"Totally understandable."

"How about you, Dad? Anyone on your radar?"

"Naw, you know me. I could never replace your mother and I don't intend to."

"But you deserve to be happy. She would want you to be."

"Naw, knowing Anne she would want me to pine for her till the end."

"Not true. You know she confided in me that she would be okay if you met somebody else. Women still love you, you know that. Just look at how the barista girl swooned over you. Why don't you ask her out?"

"She has to be thirty years my junior. What a scandal that would be."

"Brad Pitt does it, all the stars do."

My dad just chuckles, takes a bite of his sandwich, sips his coffee and looks out the window at the fall leaves tumbling across the sidewalk.

"Lets change the subject, honey, you're embarrassing me."

After a moment of silence between us I speak. "There is something I have to get off my mind. Sometimes it feels like Will is still around. I can sense him. And there is a part of me that loves, well you know, his spirit. Despite what he tried to do to me."

"You mean trying to kill you?" my father says nodding, as if he doesn't want to hear what I have to say next.

"Listen, I know you don't want to hear this because it is not the norm. But despite it all, just like you, I don't think I will ever love again. Not like that. I am just with Scott as a kind of experiment. I have needs, you know. And I am just testing the water to see if I can jump in again."

"Sylvia, you are right. And I hope you never have a love like *that* again. Because what you went through was not love. It was an aberration."

"I don't know who to tell it to. It seems nobody wants to know how I really feel."

"Let's just enjoy our food, and relax. Let me order

some more coffee."

And just like that, the conversation is over. And I feel Will in my heart, can feel him surround me like a fog of the men's cologne that his body used to permeate.

It is a scary feeling.

Dad and I continue our meals in silence and then we browse the book section of the store but don't buy any books. And then I walk him to his car.

"You've got to move on, Sylvia. Somehow you've just got to do it. And please make sure to go to that session I booked for you with the doctor."

"You mean the psychiatrist?" I say under my breath.

"Yes, it will be good for you to talk to a trained professional."

"I feel fine."

"That's what you say. But I might just know you better than you know yourself."

"I will think about it."

"Hey, its costing me a pretty penny, so please at least show up for me."

"Okay," I say. "But you know I can pay for it myself."

"Think of it as my birthday gift to you."

My dad gets in his car and shuts the door without looking at me. I slowly walk to my car and spend the next half hour driving aimlessly while listening to some sappy 80s soft rock station.

I will decide at the very last minute if I will show up for the therapy that my father has been trying to get me to go to for months. In the meantime, I can't stop thinking about the laughs and the kisses and the good times with Will. It wasn't all bad. Like eating pepperoni and pineapple pizza in bed watching horror flicks. That is until my life became one. I can see how somebody would feel betrayed if their lover or their spouse took their own life. And I also feel betrayed that he wanted to end my life. I did everything for Will. I obeyed his commands in bed. He was the dominant one, towering over me, grabbing me by the wrists and holding me down like a willing hostage. He was the one who would turn me over onto my back and slap my ass like the "bad girl" he said I was. Why did I allow him to? Why did I subjugate to his will? My safe word was "namaste." That would make him retreat when he got too rough. Most of all I loved the chemical high of our bond. It was like a bubble had formed around us.

Before I met Will I was always on the go. I had my job at the local Paint and Sip. Where I would teach the customers how to create a rose in a vase or a silly orange sunset. I knew long ago that I would never be a great artist. But I knew how to paint flowers and landscapes and I got to spread the joy of painting to those that came in and got drunk on wine and beer. I would stand in front of them and begin with telling them to spread blue across their blank white canvases. And below it green. And then we would wait for that to dry while they sipped more cheap red or white or brown. Then it was time for the tree and the owl on the branch and the moon. But after meeting Will I felt distracted on the job. I no longer wanted to be there with my beloved regulars – senior ladies who liked my delivery and how I would gently touch their shoulders when I would see how they were progressing with their amateur and slightly intoxicated works.

Now just as before, I question my desire. Imagine grieving your would-be killer. This was beyond what therapy could fix and I have always been convinced that no medication can help me cope with this. And of course living with the fact that I pulled the trigger that killed the man I loved is hard to accept.

Everyone in Grand Rapids knows my story, it was in the local papers. Which has made me consider that maybe I should move from this small city where everybody knows my name for the wrong reasons. It sure puts a hex on my dating life. What guy in his right mind would want to date the likes of me? He would have to be some kind of badass.

I could easily see it from the guy's point of view. I certainly could never date a reformed killer even if it was in self defense. And so my loneliness has deepened.

I have always been a person with a propensity towards loneliness. I was even lonely when I was with Will. Together we were like one lonely soul. We cut off all our friends. When they would call to meet for dinners or drinks we would give them all sorts of excuses and then we would stay in and make love. And sleep, and watch movies at home. And then for a time I quit my job because Will was earning enough and he would give me money. And why should I work? My desire was only to give him a child – which I never did – and to be in the throes of love.

I have my car window open, letting the cold chill of the wind swirl around me. I realize that I no longer care about my career, or building up a clientele at the company I have maintained for so many years. I no longer care to post positive affirmations on Instagram to build up my personal brand. Since I am pushing thirty I am not interested in posting videos of myself dancing on Tik-Tok. I am getting a little long in the tooth for that sort of triviality anyhow. Will never liked me posting pictures of myself online. After his death I resumed doing it again. Yet at the same time I was also more than willing to suspend all social media and lead an entirely private life. I wanted to read poetry from real books. I wanted to go for long walks and leave my smart phone at home. And most of all with that huge void in my life, I wanted to find another person to spend it with. There had to be a way to find love again. So when I went to the supermarket I would keep my ear buds out of my ears, and my eyes open for romance. I was ready to test the waters of possible love, should the opportunity arise.

I have never been a show-off in the way I present myself. Maybe I should wear black. But I don't. Even though it would be apropos since it could be said I am in mourning. I look like a modern day Jacqueline Onassis. I wear shades when I go out in public. I must send out a vibe that seems to say, "save me." But I know in my heart that I must save myself. I alone am responsible for my wellbeing.

I had been awarded money from Will's wealthy family after a successful class action settlement. His father was a prestigious cancer researcher who made a substantial fortune from grants. It nearly derailed his father's prestigious position when it came out that his son was a would-be killer. I was given hush money to go away and keep quiet. Enough to keep me comfortable for a long time. Yet I have stayed in my modest house. I have always been a homebody.

All these thoughts cascade through my mind as I pull into my driveway with those weeds punching up from the cement.

As I drive in I see it again. That car parked in front of my house. I know nothing about cars and don't know what make it is. But it looks expensive and it looks new. The thing is, it has been parked there for three days now and having it there is starting to get on my nerves. There are some college students that live a block or two down, all are crammed into an apartment with a bevy of cars overflowing in their driveway. I figure it is one of them. College kids don't care about anyone that isn't young. And I suppose, to them, I am an old crone.

I want to leave a note and put it on the car. By hand I write: *You have a nice car but you have been parked here for three days. Could you please move?* I also dialed 911 and since it is not an emergency they direct me to another annex of the police department that deals with abandoned cars. If I report the license, color and make of the vehicle then within twenty-four hours they will come out and leave a sticker on it, warning the driver to move the car within twenty-four hours or be towed. I weigh my options. I guess I am paranoid and I fear retaliation. Surely they will know I am the one who has called the cops. I don't want to be confronted by anybody anymore.

Tonight, I can hardly fall asleep even after having some warmed milk as I keep thinking about the car parked so brazenly in front of my house. There is a side of me that feels protected by it because anybody nefarious would presume I didn't live alone. And that would make it less likely that I would have a break in. I keep looking out my blinds throughout the night to see if the car is still there. As I am trying to fall asleep, if I hear a sound outside, I think it might be the vehicle owner returning.

And then comes the morning when the car is gone and you know what? I miss seeing it there. I realize it has been like a sentry for me.

All I have is me, these four walls, my dog Sweetie and my new guy who is at work. And now he is at my front door mid-shift.

Scott, my boyfriend, stands there in all his grubby glory. I do have feelings for him, make no mistake about that. Yet, I would never tell him that I loved him. It's not that sort of thing. He works hard and is a good lover. And for now that is all I am looking for. Until further notice.

As we hug I pick up on his fragrance of autumn leaves and mud. I am not sure how to describe such a scent except to say that it is earthy.

I close the door and we kiss. I can taste tobacco. I usually don't go in for smokers but I have made an exception with Scott. A girl has to overlook things if she wants a man in her life. He is an honest twenty-buck-an-hour guy. Hey, I am not saying I am paying him for his "nocturnal services." He isn't a hustler or stud. Since he owns his roofing company this is the salary he pays himself. And it is pretty good money. Anyhow, money is no object with me since I am set for years to come. But he doesn't have to know about that. In fact he seems oblivious to my reputation also. Anyway, I keep him around because a girl has needs. Anything more than that, at this point, is out of the equation.

"They say its going to rain so I have the rest of the afternoon off," Scott says, with a wide-eyed look in his eyes.

I know damn well what he wants from me.

We two don't beat around the bush.

"Okay then," I say, and I let him kiss me again.

He is already reaching under my shirt and unlatching my bra. I am not particularly in the mood this October afternoon but I can be easily enticed for a little harmless animalistic fun. This guy totally loses it when he does me. He doesn't have a self-conscious bone in his body. He lifts off my shirt and presses his mouth on and licks my tiny bit of cleavage and then he christens each of my pink, erect nipples with a kiss.

"Do you want me to shower?" he says, which makes me almost lose the vibe. After all if he is the he-man why is he asking me such a pedestrian and wimpy question at such a heated moment?

Look, I have accepted who he is, an outdoorsy guy, a man who wears Timberland boots, and walks on shingled rooftops in the hot sun. I am in this for one thing – to have a hot, human vibrator. And I have a right to pleasure. I deserve it! Because I am not the sort of girl who is ever alone. I don't do loneliness. And why should I? The guys who don't recognize me are propositioning me, from the post office lines to the hard uncomfortable plastic seats of the DMV. I want a partner. I am not a one-woman show. I like the give and take of having someone else in my life. And I certainly don't have a high tolerance for dining alone. I'd rather be sitting there with the balding bulbous loser of the year who wheezed as he ate rather than be seen on my own with a menu in my hand.

"No way," is my answer. "I want this to be dirty."

What I say really gets him going because he promptly picks me up. He is strong like that and built like that and him lifting me is always a bit of a fantasy of mine. Like being carried over the threshold in an imagined third-wedding night.

He carries me up the stairs and then he gently, playfully, throws me on my bed.

Outside I can hear the rain beginning. In fact, it really starts coming down.

He tears off my panties and almost rips off my white blouse, but thankfully it does not tear because I just got it from Amazon yesterday.

Then it is his turn. He takes off his shirt. His torso is a Greek cliché. And he unbuckles his belt and unveils his manhood.

I can only be thankful that Scott is not Will. And for now that is more than good enough.

CHAPTER FIVE

WILL

It kills me to see the two of them together on the same bed where we had once made love. For now I have to stay in limbo. Watching.

Is this my hell? Could it be that this is my inferno: to supernaturally spy on the woman I loved and married?

In the morning, after her boyfriend Scott has left, she steps into the shower and, under the hot rush of water, she sings 90s songs that really have no emotional resonance at all. She told me that she used to listen exclusively to classical music. She called it, "Meaningful symphonic music that has stood the test of time." One afternoon as we walked her dog Sweetie at Reeds Lake she told me that her mother had been enamored by the works of Chopin, Mozart and had thought that Bach's music was not only perfect but apparently mathematically symmetrical and unmatched. Her mother had always hated the pop music that was on the car radio and insisted that only classical be played. Now, with her mother dead and gone Sylvia has tried to continue listening to the great works of Tchaikovsky and Rachmaninoff but it just reminds her too much of her late mother. Now she has grown to love top forty songs as a way to escape her grief.

After her shower, Sylvia brushes her teeth with her sonic tooth brush – the one I bought her so that she could care for her blindingly white teeth. Next she plucks her eyebrows in the mirror with meticulous precision, making them pencil thin, which is her trademark look. A look that at first I thought was disconcerting. I guess I have always had a preference for women with thicker eyebrows and I had tried to get her to grow them to no avail.

As she does every morning, she now applies ample amounts of eyeliner and eyeshadow for that smokey Selena Gomez look. She is half Costa Rican and so she feels most comfortable with lips so red she could be the poster for the Rocky Horror Picture show or even the Rolling Stones logo.

My Sylvia has her usual breakfast of Columbian coffee and eggs with black beans. Now she, as always, sits at the kitchen table with her laptop and logs in to her online bank account and enters her password – which is her mother's name, Anne, followed by the year of her mother's death. Sylvia gazes at her astonishing bank balance of just under three million dollars. Paid out by my father from the civil law suit he lost. Not that he can't afford it. He still has plenty more where that came from.

Cancer research is a cash cow.

She laughs and sings an out-of-tune acapella to Hall and Oates's *Rich Girl*. Though I know she is deeply troubled inside.

All I can think about is how she stopped making love to me. Stopped wanting to have my child. Stopped wanting me. All because she said I made her feel boxed in. Caged, like a songbird. And how that tore me up inside. Until all that pent-up energy erupted like a volcano. My poisoned love was the hot lava. I wanted her to join me in hell. At least then, we could still be together. But she deflected my satanic heat.

    Now I am the only one who smolders.
    Alone.
    Banished.

is presenting as somebody with PTSD and, with her rapid speech, I would not be surprised if she has undiagnosed bi-polar disorder. But that would just be a hunch. I have a slew of standard questions for her which I'm required to ask her for this intake session. But as I feel like a talk show host with an unusually captivating celebrity guest, I decide to forget all about my preplanned questions.

I see that her particular unique predicament requires we simply have a conversation. And within this seemingly casual conversation I might best be able to decide a mode of therapy or shall I say a mode of strategy on my part. But first I need to know if she is currently taking anti-depressants or any psychotropic treatments.

"Sylvia, are you currently taking any medication?"

"Nope, don't believe in it. I want to feel everything. The ups, the downs, and the in-betweens."

"Okay, so then why don't you just tell me about yourself?" I ask, while sliding the clipboard containing my checklist of standardized questions across my desk.

"Well," she says, looking out the office window at the clouds approaching in the sky. I notice she is not meeting my eyes. "I'm not sure what to say. I guess I am a simple girl. Always have been. I was the perfect only child. I never caused my parents any trouble. I have heard that perfect girls often grow up to have all sorts of maladies. But I have done pretty well so far. I teach at local Paint and Sip. I own my own franchise."

"So you are an artist?"

"I would not call me that. I mean I can paint what I see. I have studied, you know, how to paint a decent still life or a landscape. But I have never had any ambitions to show in a gallery or any of that. I just think it's fun to paint. And I do enjoy teaching my classes, even though the clientele mostly just come to get drunk and have a good time. I am pretty good in front of people. I'm not very shy. So it has all worked out."

"'It has all worked out?'" I say, mirroring her words again.

Still she does not meet my eyes. She keeps looking at every corner of my office except at me.

"At least I thought I had it all worked out, you know. I was happily married. At least I thought so. Sure we were drifting a bit toward the end. Before it happened. I mean, I guess I started the problem when I decided we needed a little bit of a break from, you know..."

"A little bit of a break?"

"Yes, from..."

I stay silent. Giving her space to think and to find the words she wishes to use.

"From well, you know..."

Again, I don't respond.

And now she blurts out, "From . . . fucking. There I said it. Sue me."

I remain expressionless. I am not here to judge. Just to get a picture of her mental state.

"Hey, Doc, what do you think of a wife who doesn't want to fuck her husband?" she asks me.

"It doesn't matter what I think. If you did not feel like sleeping with your husband then you had every right not to. How did this affect your marriage?"

"Things were just moving too fast for me to cope."

"Things were moving too fast?" I say, mirroring her words again.

"Yes, I mean, right after we met we would get together every day. I never had a chance to catch my breath. And I guess taking a break from the sex was a way of me creating a bit of space between us."

"And how did Will respond to this sudden change of pace and the sudden lack of intimacy?"

"As expected. At first, Will was cool with it. But as I persisted in my celibacy, the tone of our relationship changed."

"And how did that make you feel?"

"He made me feel like I was doing something wrong. Like I was being a bitch."

"A bitch?"

"Yeah a real bitch. But I'm no bitch. I just needed to think things through. Our whole relationship. Things between Will and I moved very fast, right from the start. We jumped into bed within the first few hours we met. In fact we first did it on the bed at the New Year's Eve party where we met. Right under all the winter coats. And things only accelerated from there. Like I said, we never spent a day apart. It was a real rush at first. And we married four months later. Can you imagine that? And I guess in the rush of it all I had forgotten who I was. I had lost touch with my dreams."

"Your dreams?"

"My dreams are just to find out who I really am. I couldn't be me any more. I felt lost. You know, I now feel even more lost than before. Even though I have everything I need. I have a house, I have my dog, Sweetie, and a good guy for a boyfriend, for a change. Who knows, maybe I have survivor's guilt. Look, I should have died a year ago. It is a miracle that I am still here. But I don't know what do with my luck. I feel frozen in time. In that moment. When I am with Scott I . . ."

"Scott?" I ask, interrupting her, while still reflecting her words.

"That's the guy I am screwing, I mean seeing now. He's a cool person. A hard worker. But I can't seem to commit to him. I am just not sure. I guess I will never be sure. I have no fucking idea what I am doing."

She pauses and I ask, "How is your sleep?"

"Sometimes I have trouble sleeping. I have dreams about him."

"By him, I presume you mean your deceased husband?"

"Yes. I can feel Will's hands on my throat and then I wake up gasping. It totally freaks Scott out. Or I dream of Will lying there on the kitchen floor soaked in his own blood. And I know I was the one that shot him – twice. The fact I was forced to, to survive, makes no difference. I took him out of this world. And, you know, I can still feel him. Like he is still out there somewhere. I can feel him watching me. Like he is going to come back somehow and finish the job. So yeah, I wake up a few times a night and wander the house, pacing, but usually I am able to get back to sleep."

"I can offer you something for that. Would you be interested in a medication that might help you regulate your sleep pattern?"

"Hell, no. I just take some Melatonin with some hot milk. That's all I need. I'm good. I really don't want to change the chemistry of my mind."

"How is your general mood during the day?"

"Oh, well, I try to keep busy. There is so much to do, taking care of the house. Even if I am living there all alone. Endless chores. It's tiring really. I should just sell it and get a condo where everything is done for me."

Sylvia continues to describe for me the mundane routines and seemingly trivial activities of her daily life. Making breakfast, doing the dishes, laundry, walking her golden retriever, putting out the trash, shopping, going to the gym. And, as she speaks, I take in the general composure that she presents. She does not strike me as having a psychiatric illness, but I would not be surprised if she was ever so slightly hypomanic due to her moving from subject to subject without a break. Beyond that I also cannot stop myself from being taken in by her attractiveness.

She is in fact dressed slightly provocatively with a low-cut blouse that exposes her cleavage under a fashionable white sweater. I sense somehow she is consciously or unconsciously trying to draw me into the sensual aura of her presence. I might even say she is trying to seduce me with her whispery, winsome tone of voice and by crossing and uncrossing her legs and by touching her hair flirtatiously and every so often caressing her bare knees.

Even though I am her psychiatrist I am not immune to her apparent charms. But as she settles into the rhythm of her common complaints it seems she is allowing her precocious personality to bloom before my eyes. It is as if she knows that what she is talking about is of no importance. Like she is just a single woman complaining about living alone in West Michigan and the challenges therein. Yet there is a double message going on under the surface. I feel like she is dog-whistling my inner male urges as she adjusts her ass in her chair and closes her eyes as she speaks. And I am beginning to lose track of what is happening here.

It occurs to me that perhaps what she is expressing to me is that she is first and foremost a sexual being – a woman who must always keep herself sexually active with a partner and clearly never wants to resort to self-stimulation. She seems to be trying to tell me that she is a woman who desires to always have a sexual partner. It is clear that being sexually active is mandatory in her life.

And yet she expresses undeniable alienation towards her current boyfriend, Scott. It is as if she is going through the motions of her current relationship solely to have a sense of completeness. As if she has to make sure that all her ducks are in a row. Which then brings up the pertinent question as to what she truly is looking for in life, or in a man? And by sending out these signals that she is sexually satiated and satisfied then is this all to fill some other void?

It becomes apparent to me that she sends off signals to men – and that now includes me – as a kind of subconscious challenge for us to in turn step up to the plate and compete for a chance to be the one who would make her search no further. And that she includes me as one of those possible sexual male suiters.

Of course this is all conjecture on my part. And there is a chance that I myself am projecting, considering I have in my proximity a highly attractive young woman on the day she turns thirty. She is playing into my vulnerability simply because I am a man who is being paid to sit and listen to her list her emotional ailments. Possibly, this is a game she always plays. This constant call, if you will, to men, might just be a pleasurable pastime for her as well as a burden.

I discover I am gazing at the nape of her neck, or at her moving moist lips, and then as I allow my eyes to slowly wander about her body, I know that her little game is getting under my professional composure and compromising my ability to fully counsel her.

There is obviously some transference happening here. And that transference might be on my part. My thoughts are escaping me. And I begin to fantasize as to what it might be like to proposition her should I run into her outside the office.

How would a sexual encounter with her differ from my encounters with my wife?

I have been happily married for decades – yet I cannot get out of my mind what it might be like to – well, there is no other way to put it – fuck Sylvia with complete and total abandon.

My mind plunges forward with thoughts of committing adultery in a most sordid way until the veins in my neck pop as I picture myself with this woman. I envision us getting naked and worked up to sauna-like sweat. I see flashes of us climaxing in unison in some hotel suite where it would not matter how much noise we made in our ecstasy. And then afterward, calling room service and dining on hot buttered lobster. And then I gasp and catch myself mid-fantasy and realize that Sylvia has stopped talking.

"So, Doc," she says in an amusing tone, "am I ready for the funny farm or what?"

I laugh, and write some unintelligible scribbled nonsense in my notebook and say, "Well, looks like this is the end of our session. I can prescribe for you some Ambien for sleep if you would like?"

"No, that's okay. My mother used to take it. It just used to make her sleepwalk."

"Okay. To be honest, Sylvia, I really don't see any need to schedule any further appointments if you are unwilling to take medication. However I can refer you to one of our therapists to help you with your ambiguity."

"Let me think about it."

"You do that, Sylvia."

"May I go now?"

"Yes, you may. It has been a delight to meet you and I do wish you the best of luck."

"So that's it?"

"Yes, that's it."

We both get up and she extends her hand like a princess might as though she is daring me to kiss the top of her hand. Instead, I loosely shake her hand and open the door for her. We step outside, where my assistant sits at her desk.

"Sylvia does not have to be rescheduled for another appointment."

"Perfect," my assistant says, smiling.

"Bye," Sylvia says to me.

As she walks to the exit I feel shaken to my core. I also notice that a piece of paper has fallen out of her purse. I pick it up and see it is a phone bill. On it is her address. At first, I think I might catch up to her and return it. But then I think I might just like to hold on to this pertinent piece of information for myself. I can use this when the time is right.

CHAPTER SEVEN

SYLVIA

Sometimes, when I am painting with watercolors I will find that I have depicted my late husband, Will's, features and it will frighten me and I will purposely smear the colors so that they bleed into each other, creating a monstrous-looking mess which will scare me even more. It has just happened again and so I throw out the work on paper, catch my breath, and put on some coffee. Then I light up a joint to recover.

Look, I never said I have any heart-stopping talent. I know my standing as an artist. But I find painting in watercolors and acrylics to be therapeutic. It calms my nerves which have been utterly frayed for this past year. And weed helps too. It relaxes me. It takes the edge off, this morning, as the sun shines. No rain today.

I switch on my laptop and check my balance to make sure I am still okay. It is my only protection against the elements.

Is having almost three million dollars still considered rich?

Perhaps not compared to a Bezos or Branson and I am sure if I was smart there would be a way I could invest this money to make it grow exponentially.

Instead, I continue to stay in this small house where my husband died and I spend my money in a frugal manner. I prefer to just have it there in my savings account. My nest egg. Protecting me just in case something happens and I need to dip into it.

Maybe my painting is not going well because Scott and I have been fighting lately. He wants more of a commitment from me. Namely, he wants to marry me. He doesn't hide that fact and he is quite persistent. He hasn't taken it so far as to get on one knee and offer me an engagement ring. It is more of a topic of (hypothetical) discussion. The problem is, I want him but don't need him. I want his attention, and his gruff manly presence and he is good in bed, I will give him that. But I will be perfectly frank: he is not what I am looking for. Despite the trying to shoot me dead part, my departed husband was superior to my current boyfriend Scott in every way. Will believed Bob Dylan was a poet and that old people are terribly underrated members of society. His political views were radical, he believed that Los Angeles should be another country altogether. He was born in LA and he kept wanting me to move there with him. He said I would love the warm feel of the Santa Ana winds and that we could walk the Santa Monica boardwalk and drink cheap beer. He also begged me to have a baby. I am not sure what my reluctance was in the baby department. Hey, there was something I could have worked out with the oh-so-very lecherous Dr. Meadows. Oh, I very much noticed his wandering, probing eyes. I know men. Even older men. Their gaze is tangible to me. I can feel it when they fuck me with their eyes. And when the doctor shook my hand he was clearly finger-fucking me in his head. The harder that Dr. Meadows tried to conceal it with a professional demeanor, the more I knew.

I am very much aware that there is not much to be accomplished by me seeing a psychiatrist or psychotherapist. How can they understand my plight anyhow?

After getting high, I take a long hot shower and begin my day. I drive to the Woodland Mall and wander with the other shoppers. I stop at Old Navy and buy a pair of cute skinny jeans. I'm still a bit high and everything seems laughable – the young couples holding hands, the families, the father chasing his little boy who has escaped and is heading towards the kiosk with the colorful hard candy, the boomers walking with their elderly parents. The circle of life set to top forty music piping from unseen speakers. I suppose they are gearing up for the holiday season.

Has anybody at this mall seen the horrors I have seen? Has anyone looked into the eyes of death and the barrel of a loaded gun?

I don't think so.

I get myself a sub sandwich at the food quart and down it with some Diet Coke. Some random middle-aged guy tries to pick me up but I tell him I am waiting for my husband and that he should be here any minute.

Where is my future husband? That is the question. He is certainly not good-hearted, hard working Will. Can I really find the man I am looking for in Grand Rapids? And if I did meet him would his net worth measure up to my settlement windfall?

Knowing the twists and turns of love I would surely want to sign a prenup. I cannot jeopardize my golden (nest) egg. I plan to live off it for the rest of my life. My biggest fear of leaving good ole Scott is that with my luck I will meet another psycho.

Once a psycho-magnet, always a psycho-magnet.

I decide to go to the supermarket. There, I am saturated in fluorescent light. I see plump, tired mommies pushing carts filled with groceries and their offspring, dressed down, hoping to be inconspicuous. Yet even in extra-large hoodies their skin-tight leggings tell another tale. As if to say, "You can check out my ass. But leave it at that." I see an old woman in a wheelchair, who has a tracheostomy in her windpipe. She speaks through an electrolarynx, which gives her a frighteningly masculine electronic voice. The cashier asks if she wants paper or plastic for her groceries. And the old woman says, "Yes," like Darth Vader.

In the parking lot I load up my trunk with my bags of groceries as a haggard-looking, long-haired homeless guy appears out of nowhere.

"Can you help me?" he asks, knowing damn well he has scared the shit out of me.

Shaken, I give him a couple of bucks anyway. Even though I don't appreciate his shock-value method. His body odor lingers as I get in my car. I roll down the windows and, driving home, detour through the Woodlawn cemetery. And I'm not sure why. And I think about it again. My own death. Turning thirty for me is like the entrance to the beginning of the end. I am already a widow. And still unsure of what I want with what's left of my life.

My dad often says, "If you don't do something with your life. Life will do something to you."

I park my car at the cemetery, despite the fact that my frozen goods are melting. The cemetery is deserted. I walk past the gravestones that have flowers adorning them.

My mother was very much against burials. She always used to say it was a waste of space. And so, my dad and I promised her that we would cremate her but we went against her wishes and buried her here. It was my father's idea and I felt it was a betrayal and yet I felt grateful that there was a place I could go to and just be with her for a while.

I feel tears fill my eyes as I think of the pain and delirium of her last days. And that last night I sat at her bedside in vigil.

The wind picks up, tossing leaves that swirl through the air. This makes me feel so alive. My mother only wished the best for me. I have always felt that my parents were waiting for something when it came to me. Waiting for my life to take flight. And for a time, they were happy when I married Will. He made them laugh when he acted like such a kook at Thanksgiving dinners, telling complex, long-winded jokes that often ended in God-awful puns. He drank ample amounts of red wine and was often the center of attention.

I smile briefly, just thinking about him.

I arrive at my mother's gravestone. It reads: Anne Henderson, born in 1969. I never liked to think about or repeat the day that she died. It is just far too much for me to take. I feel perhaps there was something wrong about the way I was brought up. I think they cherished me too much. They never warned me of the thorns on the pretty rose that was my life on this earth. They expected nothing of me. They were just proud that I was healthy and that I was always smiling, laughing. I wished they had wanted more of me. Demanded more.

I sit against my mother's gravestone and eat the Subway sandwich I had purchased at the grocery store. I come here often and it feels good to be within her proximity. I try not to think of her body still decomposing in a coffin below. She needs these visits as much as I do. There has always been a powerful bond between us, since we were the only two women of the house. My poor father outnumbered.

"Anne," I say, because towards the end of her life I had stopped calling her mom as I saw her more as my best friend, "I wish you were here with me. I wish I could have gotten you a sandwich too. Though you always used to say that Subway's bread is way too sugary. I know it's time that I stop feeling guilty just for being alive. There has got to be a reason my life was spared. I wish you where here to help me discover it."

And then I take a bite of my turkey sandwich. I savor the taste of extra Swiss cheese. I sip my soda and wait for an answer that never comes.

CHAPTER EIGHT

ANNE

It breaks my heart each and every time Sylvia visits my grave. Especially today. Thirty years ago, I gave birth to her, my only child.

Mostly, it is just frustrating that when she speaks to me, I cannot answer her. I just want to wish her a happy birthday, tell her I love her and that everything is going to be okay. Even though I don't know that to be so.

After finishing her lunch she nods off at my graveside and sleeps for a while. The autumn leaves fall around her. I don't want her to catch a cold in the cool October breeze. Winter is calling. Just as death had called for me. I reach down to touch her soft brown hair which the wind has blown into her face. But I cannot touch and feel her any longer.

A chilly gust of wind wakes my Sylvia and she kisses my gravestone and gathers up her things and walks back to her car.

I follow her to her car like the cosmic drone that I am and when she arrives back at her house I can see that godforsaken car parked on the street fronting her house. I used to have a pet peeve when any stranger's car parked in front of our family home. I would leave a note or call the damn cops if I were her.

I wonder who it is that is so inconsiderate as to behave as though this is a public parking spot. She walks around the car, examining it. It's a black Porsche. I know she is wondering why someone keeps parking in front of her home. Questioning why they don't fuck off elsewhere. Finally, she goes inside her lonely home. How I wish, with all her money, she would leave that little fixer-upper. Maybe just leave Grand Rapids altogether. If I were her and I was young, beautiful and alive I would move out to the west coast, earthquakes and fires be damned. That's the price you pay for paradise.

She prepares for herself a T-bone steak while listening to some God-awful pop rock station. How I wish she still listened to classical music, something we once shared enjoyment in. I can't help but feel she is betraying me. But I understand that listening to it might cause her to miss me that much more. She pops open a bottle of red wine and, before long, she is getting tipsy as she spreads garlic on the juicy steak that sizzles in the hot iron pan. And then she moves slowly around the room. Dancing all by her lonesome.

Good, at least she is content. Even if she is alone.

Her cell phone rings and she picks it up. I can hear his voice well enough.

"Hey, it's me."

"Hiya, Scott."

"Watcha doin'?"

"Having a dose of protein and spirits."

"Sounds good. So are we still on for tonight? Are you still looking for any company on your birthday. I can bring more wine."

"Naw, bring tequila. I could use a shot or two."

"Anything else?"

"Just your hot bod and some mint chip Haagen-

Dazs. Do ya want me to throw on another steak for you?"

"Naw, I already ate. I am just hungry for you?"

"Really? Now?"

"When I get there I just want to eat you up. You taste so good."

"You are just chock-full of sexy compliments. I will see you soon."

"Can I say it?"

"No, we have an agreement."

"I'd like to break the rules."

"Please don't start."

"Okay, I don't want to fight."

Scott ended the call.

I know what they are squabbling about because I have heard it all before. Sylvia doesn't want to voice: "I love you." And truly, I wish she was not being so stubborn. Scott is a nice enough guy. Sure he is not a Rockefeller, but he has a good steady job. He owns his own business and seems to genuinely care about her.

After what has happened to her, and what she has done, what is it going to take for her to settle down?

I am fading again. I don't seem to have long in this give and take, push and pull, appear and disappear relationship I have with the living.

When will I next be able to slip through time, space and mortality to visit my daughter?

CHAPTER NINE

SCOTT

For once, I don't want to screw this thing up. I have found a keeper in Sylvia and I plan on doing everything in my power to make our relationship work. This woman has something about her that not only turns me on but also makes me want to look after her. To take care of her. She thinks I don't know, but I know everything about her. Everybody in town does. Does not phase me in the least. Not many chicks would be able to get ahold of a killer's gun and shoot them before they were able to kill. More power to her. I ain't getting any younger. And I have been through a few women in my time. Some loose cannons and some crazed bitches and a few that I let slip through my fingers because I was too busy to notice I was losing them.

I'm driving my pickup to Sylvia's place and I'm thinking that shit, maybe I really am some sort of workaholic?

Look, I want to own my house rather than keep on paying rent. And I don't mean I want my bank to own it. I want to own it outright. And yeah I want to stay here in Grand Rapids. This is a good place to raise a family. Did I say family? Oops, I let that slip, but yeah,

I would not mind if I got Sylvia in the family way. Maybe have a max of three kids. Three is an odd number but I have always thought three of 'em would be just right. I'm kinda ready to be a family man. I have no qualms about girls but I got my heart set on a boy. I'd like to teach him how to ride a bike, how to change the oil in a car. And, you know, compete in a little local college football.

Go Blue!

Look, I ain't perfect. I fully admit I have fucked up a few things in my life. My folks are disappointed in me. They have never been that proud of me and my roofing company. They wanted me to end up like my brother who is Mr. Smarty pants. He is the one with a degree. He's the one who lives in Lancing with a wife and two perfect kids. And has a good job at a law firm. We are so very different. Like oil and water. I was the one who liked to get his hands dirty and he liked to keep them clean. I was the one chasing tail while he hit the text books. And more power to him! We have always been two very different people. I started getting into trouble. You know, I fell into petty thievery and started getting drunk and a little high. I bet right now he is in his office looking over a contract while his sassy-ass assistant brings him coffee. He has it made in the shade. And hell, on the salary I give myself, I can't even manage to own my own home. But I will show him and I will show our folks before they go to the great beyond that I can make good. I will get the girl – Sylvia! I will get the house and the white picket fence and all that jazz. But at twenty-eight, I feel like time is slipping away from me. My back aches from stooping over on rooftops and hammering all day. It hurts when I make love to Sylvia.

I arrive at the front door of her house. She opens

the door, I step inside and wish her a happy birthday and we embrace. She holds me so tight that it triggers some spasms in my spine but I never let on. She doesn't need to know that my back-breaking work has brought on chronic arthritic pain. And I am in no position to treat it. I have no medical insurance. In any case her touch is always healing.

"I am so happy you are here," she says, after we kiss.

"Yeah, I'm glad to have the afternoon off."

"You seem tired," she says, looking me over.

I never want to show her my weakness. My pain is mine alone. One day when the business is doing better maybe I will invest in myself and get some scans and get to the bottom of it. But for now I am willing to just suck it up and keep trucking.

"Do you want to eat or should we just do it? After all, I am the birthday girl." She smiles playfully, her teeth bright white.

I reply with a kiss to the nape of her neck, which she responds to by biting my ear. It ain't long before we are making our way up those steps yet again. There is a good chance that without well, fucking – how else can I put it? – we wouldn't have much to talk about. After all she is mostly a delicate woman, who teaches painting classes, and likes to binge on romcoms and the occasional supermarket paperback romance. Other than that I can't say I know much about who she really is. I have met her father, Harold, the widower, and he is a good man. He has never shown any disapproval of me. In fact, I sense he just seems anxious for me to get it over with and get hitched to his daughter and make an honest woman out of her before she becomes an old maid.

We strip in a hurry as if the house were about to burn down and we were trapped and these were our last moments on earth. As I kiss her up and down her body, I feel her quiver with wild energy. I'll be damned if this woman knows how lucky she is to still be alive and she wants to make the most out of it any way she can.

Look, I know she is using me much more than I am using her. She thrives on sensations, hard kisses. She wants to eat as much as she can – she never gains – though perhaps you might say she has thighs on the thicker side, which I find amazingly hot. It culminates in her apple-shaped ass.

She has turned on her Pandora radio and *Focus* by H.E.R comes on. A sexy adult R&B song. A sultry female voice demands sole attention. And that is what I am doing yet again. Always making sure that Sylvia comes first. And as I kiss her between her legs I look up and see that she quivers. There is a sensual sadness about her that makes a guy like me want to save her. After bringing her to this first climax, I climb on top of her and enter her and she looks away from me as I thrust into her, alternating between biting her lips and opening them to take in some air. Then she sighs in the same key as the music's lyrical note.

Making love is how we spend her birthday. After, she says she wants to shower alone, that is if I don't mind. I tell her that I don't. After her shower we drink wine in bed and talk.

"So how was your day?" she asks.

"You should know, I'm spending it with you."

"I mean your morning and afternoon."

"Well, if we got married and you moved in with me you would know."

"Ha, funny, there you go pressuring me again. You know I can never give up this house."

"You know I'm just pressing your buttons."

"If you are going to insist on pressing my buttons, just press the ones between my legs."
"My pleasure."
"You're good at that."
"Good at what?"
"Pressing my buttons."
"Thanks."
"Have you heard that before?"
"I plead the fifth."
"Smart guy."
"Not that smart."
"Sure you are. I'm serious now. I mean you have your own business and all. I think you are going to be a wealthy man one day."

This is a back-handed compliment as she is acknowledging the fact that right now I am just making ends meet. I wonder if this is why she doesn't want to tie the knot with me. This makes me angry inside. I will never show it. I put the bread on the table. I pay the bills, I change my own tires, I balance my personal bank accounts as well as do the accounting for my company. I may not be where I thought I would be by now, but maybe in a few years all this sweat and blood and back pain will pay off and I will be on easy street. And I want Sylvia by my side and along for the ride. And I am the kind of sonofabitch that gets what he wants. I get the girl. Always have.

Sylvia and I snack on cold fried chicken wings. We eat mint chip ice cream. She tells me that there was a car parked in front of her house for a while but is now gone. I ask her what kind of car and she says she believes it might have been a Porsche. She asks me if she should call the cops or leave a note and said she sees it as an omen of bad things to come.

"What if seeing a black Porsche in front of your

house is the same as seeing a black cat cross in front of you?" she asks.

"No way, I would see it as a sign that good things are in store for you. Anyhow if it parks there again I will knock on a few of your neighbors doors and see who is behind this fucking invasion of privacy."

"Now you are just teasing me."

"Well, what about it bothers you?"

"In the morning I like to sip my mug of coffee and look out my living room window. And it pisses me off if a car is there."

"Tell me if you spot it again and I will take care of the situation."

"You are not going to puncture the tires or key the car are you?" she jokes.

"To a Porsche? No fucking way. I am sure whoever it is, is just an entitled rich dude."

"It might be a woman."

"It might."

"You don't sound very convinced that it would be a woman."

"Let's not fight."

"Come on, that is like totally misogynistic for you to think that a woman wouldn't drive a fancy car."

"Okay, cool your jets. Let's watch a flick."

"Okay, but nothing scary."

She never wants to watch horror flicks or thriller flicks. Nothing with guns. Nothing with blood. Nothing with murder. It is all still too soon for her.

"You know, Sylvia, you probably have PTSD. You really should seek therapy for it. There is no stigma to it anymore.

"Please don't start. My dad finally got me to go see a psychiatrist. I went to the guy today and he was a total creep. I will never go back."

"What was so creepy about him?"

"Oh, I don't know, maybe just the way he stared at me."

That's what psychiatrists do. They listen and observe from the little I know."

"I don't want to talk about it, Scott. Okay?" She gives me a tender kiss on the lips. "Please promise me we won't talk about it any more."

"I promise. But just so you know, if any guy looks at you the wrong way tell me and I will take care of the situation."

CHAPTER TEN

DR MEADOWS

As a trained medical professional it is my job to assess the human psyche, sometimes in under thirty minutes, and prescribe for them a drug that will alter their brain chemistry. And so, having so little time with my clients, I have to rely on quick judgments based on what little I observe. Yet it is I who feels off-balance. Sleep has become a problem and that is always a red flag. Tonight, I wake at 3 a.m. after a vivid dream. I don't want to disturb my wife and so I quietly get out of bed. I am so riled up that I feel I might not be able to get back to sleep. I realize that I am meant to be in work in the morning, and who am I kidding if I think I can do my job on half a night's sleep?

Yes, sleep. Nighttime workaholics scuff at sleep as if it is unneeded. Illicit drug users high on stimulants like meth or cocaine think it's quite alright to go two days without any REM. But my theory is that dreaming offers a release for the subconscious to work out its issues. I am well aware that it is common to have dreams about people we have met. I just did. It was an erotic smorgasbord that involved me fucking the shit out someone. This is the mind's way of fleshing out subconscious fantasies. Nature's LSD. The human brain has the ability to supply much-needed nocturnal porn on demand. I feel deeply ashamed that I saw visions in my dreams of unimaginable and sordid sexual acts with Sylvia. I cannot even bare to say what it is we did.

Would a midnight snack soothe this suddenly savage beast? Sure, why not?

I open the door to the fridge which my wife keeps stocked at all times. She loves spending my money. She clearly went shopping while I was at work. I decide on a bagel with cream cheese and lox. I toast the bagel and when it is ready I spread the cream cheese on each half and begin to chew. I am famished. I devour the sesame bagel. After I am done, I find I'm still hungry. So I take out one of those store bought roast chickens and I break off a leg and thigh and eat it like a caveman standing at the kitchen counter.

I consider the people whose problems I've listened to over the years and have the sudden realization that my inability to sleep might be due to the obsession that's formulating within me. Another red flag.

Sylvia's history and her temperament touched me in ways I never expected. I have never treated a woman who has killed her husband. I know, from having treated veterans, how both empowering, liberating and yet also debilitating taking a life can be. I have been told that at the moment when the bullet shoots from the barrel there is a feeling unlike any other. A kind of flesh-searing dominance over one's enemy and then in the aftermath comes the realization that one has played God. And that perhaps God might be angry. To put it mildly, from my clinical experience it eats away at you, and never lets up.

Fear of God's wrath. It can eat a person alive.

Sylvia vexes me. I had already arranged for some extensive research into her personal life before our first appointment. I want to be a part of Miss Sylvia Henderson's recovery. But how? Since I ended any chance of us having a professional relationship by telling her that unless she took medication I couldn't help her. How stupid of me.

What kind of self-sabotage was that?

Must I wait for fate to intervene till we meet again?

I have her address. She lives on the cusp of East Grand Rapids and I live in one of the more prestigious addresses in East Grand rapids proper. Often voted as the ideal place to raise children. Which I have successfully done. My son turned out just fine. He is roughly Sylvia's age, and, to be honest, he would be better suited to date her than me. Protocol would probably dictate that introducing them would be overstepping my ethical boundaries. It simply would not be appropriate. Neither is it appropriate for me to be fixating on her as I do. Which though I have tried to conceal, to deny, I must admit I'm finding difficult.

CHAPTER ELEVEN

ANNE

When she was a child Sylvia was not totally aware of the difficulties I had with her father, Harold. We had a marriage that felt like it was built on a foundation of hot coals. I was a headstrong woman who was not afraid to talk back and he was a sometimes infuriating man and the two of us argued about everything from Christmas toys – whether we should spend a fortune and spoil our only child, or be more frugal considering his position at the University brought in only a modest wage. I stayed with Harold because he was such a good father to Sylvia.

I watch as she walks her dog, Sweetie, over at Reeds Lake. With her black turtleneck sweater and her bright red schoolgirl-style mini-skirt and her red knee-high socks she has a Mod retro-fashion flare, like she has just stepped out of *Life* magazine, circa 1960. She looks like a Kodachrome snapshot.

An unassumingly handsome man approaches and compliments her.

"Do you always doll yourself up like this?" he says.

"RuPaul says everyone is in drag. What we wear says a lot about ourselves."

"What does what I wear say about me?" this

stranger asks.

"Well, you are dressed in jeans and a matching jean jacket so I would say you are a casual guy that does not give a shit about the way that you come across. I wouldn't call you slovenly but I would call you laid-back."

"Is that a good or a bad thing?"

"Depends on what is happening. If I wanted to attend the Lyric Opera house in Chicago to see *The Ring* you would not be my first choice if you intended to dress like that."

"You mean the ushers wouldn't let me in like this?"

"Maybe not. You would stand out like a sore thumb."

"How about if I dressed like this when we go dine in McDonalds?"

"I prefer more fine dining than that, thank you."

"You sound like high-maintenance."

"Not at all. I like to pay my way. Unless a man insists."

"Are you wondering if I would insist?"

"No, because there is no way that I would ever go out with you. I already have a man."

"How serious is it?"

"Serious enough for me to bring it up in the first few minutes of our conversation."

"I guess I should take a hint."

She pauses, and then says, "You give up too easily."

I know she says this because she sees something in this stranger by the lake. He is a tall man and there is something classy about him. He is nothing like Scott. Scott is a working man. This guy looks upscale. Not like the bad boys that my girl used to fall for and who brought us nothing but grief. I remember the boys on motorcycles arriving at our house handing her a helmet and telling her to "hop on." They would take her to nightclubs and would not return her to the house till dawn's early light, with her hair disheveled, her blouse wine-stained and her mascara running. And here is another guy who seems to appear out of the blue. Cowboy boots and all. He may not have a southern snarl, but he has the smartass smirk of a big city gunslinger.

Why the hell she agrees to go out to lunch with this complete and total stranger is upsetting. And that is when I step away and cannot watch any more. I mean she already has Scott, a perfectly good catch. And now she has to muck it up with another guy.

Sometimes I just don't understand my Sylvia.

CHAPTER TWELVE

SYLVIA

I know what I am doing. I may not really know anything about this guy except his name is Hank. But I like his energy. I can tell he is a mover and a shaker. And my life is in desperate need of some shaking up. He gives Sweetie and I a ride back to my place in a plush luxury car that he says is a rental. During the ride he tells me dinner will be on him. I ask that we just go to a cheap place as I much prefer cheap food.

"If you insist," he says, with a sly smile.

After I drop Sweetie off at my place this Hank guy drives me to Red Robin at the Woodland Mall. A family friendly hamburger and fries emporium. The more time I spend with him the more he comes off like some sort of David Geffen in disguise. Isn't it true that all the billionaires like to dress down? Like Zuckerberg with his trademark grey T-Shirt. I know it by this guy's Rolex watch, I know it by the diamond earring he wears that signals his flamboyant wealth. His blue eyes catch the afternoon light and sparkle. I am intrigued.

I am about to ask him a series of surgically precise questions when our tall, slender, black waitress with the blue eyeshadow and blue lips approaches our table. She has skinny, exotic model runway looks.

"What is an elegant girl like you doing in a joint like this? Heck what are you doing in a town like this?" Hank asks our hot waitress.

"Believe me, I would quit here if I could," she says.

"Somebody famous, once said, there is a Greyhound bus leaving every hour. Girl, you could get first place on that *Project Runway* show."

"Pretty girls are a dime a dozen," she says with youthful bitterness. "I hear it's a cutthroat industry. Not sure if I could handle it."

"I can make a few calls for you. I know some people over at Ford. Here's my card. I'd be happy to help. In the meantime I will have a bacon burger and ice water. Sylvia, what will you have?"

"Grilled chicken burger with fries and a Diet Coke, please."

"Naw scratch her Coke order. Sylvia, what do you say we have real drinks?" Hank asks. "You guys make margaritas here, right?"

"We sure do," our waitress replies.

"Give us two strawberry margaritas. I will have salt on mine. And you Sylvia?"

I agree with Hank. It is high time for some liquor.

"I'll have mine with salt as well," I say.

The waitress smiles, takes our menus and walks off. She is a beauty and it was nice of Hank to make her night with his compliments.

"I'm glad you have accepted my invite to this early dinner, considering we just met. Thank you for trusting me."

"It's not a matter of trust. I am doing it because this girl is hungry."

"Good. I like a girl with a healthy appetite."

He keeps throwing double entendres at me like they are going out of style. He does have a way about him. A cool confidence. Though he might be a little too slick for my taste.

"You do now?" I ask.

"Yes, I do. Anyway I want to know more about you."

"I'd rather talk about you first. What do you do for a living?" I hope I am not being too assertive."

"Well, I guess you aren't messing around. Well, in a nutshell I am a man who builds brand platforms. I guess you could say I am in publicity. Though these days we work more with influencers than we do with advertisers. If we can get our clients to be a part of a viral post it can do wonders for their bottom line. I was ahead of the curve and well, I just got lucky."

"So you run a kind of PR agency? Who do you represent?"

"A very popular scented candle company out of the Pacific Palisades in LA. And a few wineries in Tuscany, as well as some up and coming celebs on the East Coast. Not the kind of celebs who sing or act per say. Just Tik-Tok and Instagram personalities that do nothing more than know how to make their lives seem visually appealing. You see, I like people who have interesting lives. People who can make brewing a cup of coffee in the morning somehow appear special. People who can discuss just about anything and yet be highly watchable and likable. They are hard to find. I have to comb the internet to find them. But I find them and I make them even more sensational than they already are. The only thing that changes in their life is that I take my percentage and they can do whatever they fucking want with the rest."

"I have never heard of such a business. So are you a talent scout?" I ask, as our sexy, high-fashion waitress brings us our oversized, artificially, strawberry-colored Margaritas.

"Like I said, I am not looking for talent. I am looking for people with a timely spark. Relevant people. People that manage to have their finger on the pulse of the moment."

I sip my margarita. And the more I sip the more it feels somehow things are falling into place for me. I no longer see Hank as a complete stranger. Instead, I feel like he is about to escort me into a glittery new life. And I feel open to go where this leads. I need this. I really do. It just feels right. And I am willing to let my guard down and just trust. And yeah, go with it.

CHAPTER THIRTEEN

ANNE

I can only watch over my dear daughter on and off. I don't understand this abyss I am in. It seems I am always in flux. I am now, once again, watching what she is up to and I don't trust this Hank guy. And there is nothing I can do about it.

It is utterly reckless of her to agree to have dinner with this guy she meets at Reeds Lake.

She has always been such an impetuous girl. When she met Will it was all hot and heavy, a rush from the start. The two of them were positively high on youthful hormones and endorphins and I am sure plenty of sex. Taking up with Will, that pseudo-intellectual professor of English Lit at the local community collage, was her only, almost fatal, mistake.

When my husband and I would spend an evening with them and take in a movie, Will would never tolerate seeing a Hollywood blockbuster. He would always insist we go to a lesser known arthouse foreign film.

My husband and I despised subtitles due to our failing eyesight, yet we tried to keep the peace and endure some French movie with a tragic ending or solemn Swedish film set mostly in snowy landscapes with stern faces, that dealt with love and death in equal measure. After the show Will would insist that we skip the chain restaurant and instead support a locally-owned one that was overpriced with lousy service and questionable entrees, like braised beef that often arrived at our table cold. Harold could not tolerate strange meals and would just ask for a bowl of fresh fruit. And, oh, the insufferable table talk! It always had to be about Russian authors or dreaded politics. We considered ourselves to be left wing but Will was a proud semi-socialist to whom Marx and Che Guevara were cult superstars. Will never did know how to go with the flow. He had to counter everything, debate or disagree. And my husband and I would be utterly exhausted by it all. I think the stress contributed to my cancer of the spine. I just never took to Will. And as it turned out I was oh so right.

Now, once again, there is nothing I can do to alter Sylvia's fate. My hands are tied. I am only a vapor. So very useless and pathetic. You might as well throw a sheet over me and send me out trick or treating on Halloween.

All I can do is wonder who this new man is who has so suddenly come into my Sylvia's little world.

CHAPTER FOURTEEN

HANK

She doesn't know this is all no accident. This chance meeting at the quaint little lake. She has been going there for many weeks to walk her dog. I know all about her. I find this petite, yet shapely young woman with the thick brown hair and dark bewitching eyes positively irresistible. Yet sparking a romance is not my intension. This, for the time being, is strictly professional. I see something in Sylvia. A raw potential to affect the masses. Women mostly.

Her name is no longer in the media. She was a blood-stained flash in the pan. Yet while she shined, she shined with deadly effervescence.

I know for a fact that many women in the US still consider her a role model. She is a woman who stood up to her abuser in the most existential way. She took her evil husband's power away, namely his gun, and used it against him. Women love her and she scares men. Just as Lorena Bobbitt once scared men. Sylvia spooks many gun owners. And I like that. I want to exploit it to the nth degree. I just need to find the right product for her to get behind. We represent a few male and female antiperspirant brands but this might be too edgy for them. Maybe a gun dealership?

Well, that might be too obvious and I don't want to cater to those who are gung-ho gun enthusiasts.

Sylvia Henderson is the anti Greta Thunberg. She is one badass babe and just maybe, with her disarmingly soft-spoken tone of voice, she could be the spokeswoman for a home protection company. Or maybe not. I have been thinking a line of women's wear with T shirts that sport slogans like: I'm no Victim; Killer Abs; F with Another Woman; Don't F with Me, and so on. She is a potential cash cow. I believe the shock of her act of self-preservation has subsided and maybe the public at large can laugh a little with her. I'd like to see how she does on the talk show circuit. She would kill on *Stern*. But we'd have to work up to that. And then once I have made her a brand name associated with woman power then I might step in and maybe take things a little further.

She is a lovely woman. And I am smitten. Just as any man would be. Good things come in small packages and there is something about Sylvia's small frame that brings out the protector in me. I'm sure many men feel the same way. In any case, there is good news, after sharing three strongly spiked margaritas I have gone ahead and proposed on the spur of the moment that she come to the big apple for a whirlwind vacation.

Her answer is, "Everything moves so fast in my life. It has always been that way for me. And I guess I like fast men. And so, yeah, I'd like to take you up on your kind invitation."

"Fantastic," I say. "I will have my assistant, Angelique, make the arrangements right away."

My plan is to wine and dine Sylvia until she is begging for more. Then I will present her with my business management contract.

My associates thought I was being crazy flying out

to Grand Rapids on a hunch. Now I no longer feel like a stalker, even though our chance meeting was all part of my plan.

CHAPTER FIFTEEN

SYLVIA

It is always heartbreaking to board Sweetie but I trust the kennel and I paid for her to have her own suite and to be groomed while I am gone. It is costing me a pretty penny, but I will spare no expense for a dog that has always felt more like my baby girl to me. As I take the Uber to the Gerald Ford Airport, I mull over memories of my stubborn reluctance to give Will a child. This was an issue of contention between us. I don't know what was holding me back. Perhaps I was more intuitive than I might have thought. With a dangerous man like that, perhaps it is a miracle that we never brought a baby into this world.

Meeting Hank has brought out my hidden ambitions. I always have felt deep inside that I am destined for greatness. Like a Wonder Woman. I guess like most girls I have fantasies some talent scout will spot me in the grocery store and sign me. I see myself in the driver's rear-view mirror and cannot help but think that at last my Svengali has come. Hank has already told me that he sees potential in me. I am going to go along for the ride and keep an open mind. I cannot go on living the way I have. Just treading water. I know I have Scott and he is a sweetheart but I am not sure he *does it* for me. Not that I am anticipating taking up with Hank. On the contrary I still have my guard up. I have already requested that I stay in my very own hotel room just down the hall from him. And that was what inspired me to pay for a suite for Sweetie.

Only the best for me. And only the best for my fur baby.

My Uber driver is from India and is he mostly silent as he speeds along the highway, keeping me on-edge. When we get to the airport he gets out of the car and takes out my carry-on luggage from the trunk. I like to travel light.

"Have good time in New York City," he says, with an accent that tells me he has traveled farther and wider than I probably ever will.

"Thanks," I say.

I roll my luggage to the entrance of the airport. I scan the crowd looking for Hank. I have not yet spotted him in the crowd of travelers. Now he appears, towing his own sleek, carry-on black luggage. Once again he is deceptively dressed down in tennis shoes, jeans and a black T-shirt, and with chains around his neck like the bass player of a classic rock band on tour. His five o'clock shadow and buzzed hair adds to his casual nouveau rich appeal.

"I see you decided not to shave?" I joke.

"Well, guess I'm not planning on getting kissed," he kids back.

I am somewhat grateful that I won't be feeling his stubbled chin grate on my sensitive cheek.

A young woman with artificially white hair dressed in a cute, retro outfit joins us. She wears heels, red leather pants and a flamboyant paisley top that is a throwback to the seventies. She looks highly presentable.

"Sylvia, meet Angelique, my assistant. She is my right-hand woman. And she will make sure that your visit to New York City goes smoothly. If there is anything that you need at any time she will be there for you."

"Greetings, Sylvia, I have heard so much about you," Angelique says, with an English accent that instantly makes her seem enchanting.

"Nice to meet you," is all I can come up with.

I could kick myself for not being a little more clever than that. Everything is moving so fast. The way I like it. Hank is like my very own younger version of Branson and his sexy assistant adds to his prestige and growing sex appeal. After all, here is a man who gets to spend all of his working hours with a well-coiffed smoking-hot woman.

"The pleasure is all mine. If you don't mind I will text you through the cell number that Hank provided. Is it okay that I have your number?" Angelique asks.

"Yes, of course, perfectly fine. You know I'm a street smart girl. I will be just fine. Heck, I could figure out a way to get by even if I was dropped in Manhattan without a credit card. I'm a survivor."

"You certainly are," Angelique says. "That is precisely why Hank is working with you now. We love survivors."

"And so will millions of other women if we do this thing right," Hank adds.

We have our tickets scanned and we are walking towards our gate. Yet, we don't head to the normal gates that everybody goes to. Instead we go through a passage that I have never seen. We walk down some more empty halls and then we exit the building and wind up walking on the tarmac towards a small, bright white private jet. I try not to show my excitement and apprehension.

Isn't it always the private planes that go down?

The aircraft has a name. The logo shows a graphically depicted eye and written in cursive in the pupil is the word: INTENTION.

They let me be the first to walk up the steps. Once I am inside I am greeted by a pretty young flight attendant. I almost gasp as I check out the posh interior of the jet. I can see that there is no such thing as business class. It is first class all the way! Plush leather seats face towards each other like this is the VIP room of a nightclub. Within seconds refreshments are being offered. Our flight attendant takes my carry-on and quickly stows it away and then she hands me a glass of sparkling champagne. I end up with a window seat. Next to me Angelique takes out her laptop while Hank scrolls on his phone across from us.

"You didn't really think we were flying commercial?" Hank asks me.

"I really had no idea."

"I told you that you are in good hands. So sit back and enjoy the ride. And cheers."

We all clink our glasses and sip our champagne.

I really have nothing to occupy myself and I regret not picking up a steamy bestseller at the airport gift shop. The two young pilots, both bearded, one with a bun in his hair, come out and introduce themselves like they are two Rave DJs instead of the two men who hold my life in their hands. The hair bun pilot asks politely if I prefer hip-hop or classic rock.

"Hip-hop," is my answer.

The two of them step inside the high-tech cockpit and within moments a current rap song comes on featuring a singer who is heavily auto-tuned.

My heart skips a beat when the airplane ascends into the clouds. I look out the circular window at the wonder of those puffs of dreamy condensation and play a game in my mind that I used to play when I was a little girl on a flight. I try to find hidden images in the clouds. I think I see the features of my mother. As if she is floating in midair like an angel in broad daylight. It startles me and makes me shiver for a moment. I contain myself. When we reach cruising altitude a pilot's voice sounds over the loudspeakers and welcomes us and tells us it should be a "smooth ride" all the way to New York City. The flight attendant rolls her cart of snacks on over to us and Hank smiles at her with a genuine warmth that I am sure melts the hearts of women.

"Why don't we all get shots of tequila and some lite beers. Are you game?" Hank asks.

"I'm game with that," Angelique says, while never looking up from her laptop.

I am not sure at first. Then I realize that Hank has the right idea. If this small plane goes down at least we will all die drunk.

"Sure," I say.

"Perfect," Hank says.

We wind up having three shots and three beers and I wind up laughing as the two of them talk about all their exploits during their travels. They casually drop the names of the exotic places they have seen from India, to the South of France, to South Africa and many more. They talk business. Angelique reads off the amount of engagements their new social media ad campaigns have gotten. One has received one hundred thousand retweets, and likes. They rarely talk about magazines or newspapers. It seems from my perspective that their focus is on social media. Angelique shows me a video clip on Tik-Tok of one of Hank's clients dancing in her bikini and there is nothing about it that makes me think this is anything special. Sure the young woman has a body to die for. But so what? Tik-Tok is overcrowded with girls willing – including me – to straddle the fine line between improvised self-choreography and soft porn.

"We represent the bikini line she is wearing and this video which has one point two million views has generated a forty percent increase in sales on Amazon. That's how it works now. Young consumers decide on what to buy next based on viral videos. They want to know what the other kids are wearing and they want to do the same."

"Cool," I say, realizing that I am getting quite tipsy.

"We would have had to spend hundreds of thousands of dollars in advertising to get this sort of buzz. But we only had to send out one hundred complimentary bikinis to trending viral Tik-Tok girls and here you have the result. It is a new world out there."

"Amazing," I say.

I now have two powerful new friends and I am managing to temporarily escape the monotony of my life and my overbearing boyfriend Scott. Though I do already miss Sweetie, I do need this getaway.

Hank has drifted off to sleep with ease. It seems he is a man who has it all and can sleep soundly at the drop of a dime. Angelique continues to work on her smartphone and her laptop. I am amazed by how dexterous she is with her impressively long red fingernails. She only seems mildly concerned with keeping me entertained during the flight.

"You can get up and stretch," she says after a time.

I take her up on that. I unbuckle my seatbelt and stand up. We are the only three passengers besides our cute flight attendant who smiles at me in anticipation of my wanting more refreshments.

There is a video screen in the rear. Magazines, like

Architecture Digest and *Vanity Fair* are stacked on game tables. I can hear and feel the hum of the engine. I can sense the sky surrounding me and all I really want to do is get even more intoxicated. I ask the flight attendant for another drink. This time I just want the shot.

She obliges saying, "Of course Sylvia, right away."

This is the first time I have been on a first name basis with a flight attendant. I down the shot and ask for another.

"What are your plans when we land in the city?" she asks.

"I have no idea. I suppose Hank is in charge of all that."

"Must be very exciting. He is a very powerful man. The sort that can change a woman's life."

"Yes, that is what I have gathered."

"I wish he took an interest in me like he does in you. I often meet his clients on the plane and it's just a vicarious thrill for me. I'm a singer myself. Mostly I just perform solo at my electric piano on Facebook live for online tips. I can sometimes get up to twenty thousand views if I show cleavage. Funny how that never happens when I keep my shirt buttoned up."

I laugh, now noticing she is full-breasted and really quite lovely.

"Are you married?" I venture to ask.

"No, most guys don't want a wife who is constantly globetrotting with millionaires. Most, if I can be candid, think I am a mile-high hooker."

"You're funny," I say.

"I have been propositioned on red-eye flights to Zurich," she says. "But I don't think it is appropriate to say 'yes' to a drunk billionaire. That's not what I am looking for anyway. The last thing I need to do is sign an air-tight prenup only to get dumped for the next hot young thing he meets in Monte Carlo."

"Yeah, I guess you are right. I suppose there are no sure things when it comes to love and money."

"Just between you and me I will tell you this. Sex goes with money. Love does not."

"I'll keep that in mind."

"Listen, Sylvia, don't let me discourage you. From what I hear, you are single and ready to mingle. So by all means keep your options open. Maybe things will work better for you than they have for me."

The plane tilts to the left and the rumbles vibrate throughout my body.

"You had better get in your seat. Looks like we have some turbulence. I'm going to buckle in myself."

I wobble to my seat and snap on my seatbelt. Angelique puts hers on as well, as she continues working on her laptop. She gives me a smile as if to reassure me that we aren't going to die together. Not now. Not like this.

I secretly pray to myself, to Jesus, and ask that should we dive down into dark, cold night that my soul is saved and that I can perhaps be placed in the same condo cloud community where my dear mother now spends eternity.

How I wish I could speak to her again. She had warned me about Will. When we first dated she had done some online research and found out that my then future husband had been arrested once because he got physical with a college girlfriend. Apparently, after suspecting her of cheating with a guy from the debate team he had tracked her down at a local watering hole and had dragged her by her hair out of the bar and shoved her around in the alley until some bouncers broke it up and called the cops.

But I refused to believe that it was true. And if it was true I didn't think it had played out as I was told.

Trolls who spread online rumors have a way of exaggerating everything. And from what I knew about Will, the only sort of sparring that he engaged in was purely verbal. And then again if it all was true I figured that maybe the girl deserved it in a way. I know it was not normal or politicly correct for a woman to side against another woman especially the victim of abuse. But from what I know of girls my age they can be little bitches. And some of them purposely do just awful things to their boyfriends just to get a rise out of them and get a little attention. I know far too many couples who fight and fuck. It's a vicious circle. The arguing is foreplay.

After a few scary minutes the plane rights itself. And I allow my thoughts to settle. I once again try to bask in the mid-air luxury and my pleasant high-end company.

"Did that put a scare in you?" Hank asks me, with his bleached white smile.

"A little, I must admit."

"My pilots are world-class. I promise you we will get you to New York City fully intact."

"Thank you."

With that, he signals for the flight attendant to bring us menus. We have a choice of seared lamb with potatoes or Cornish hen. I choose the hen. She brings our meals within minutes, piping hot and smelling delicious.

I devour my meal quickly. I guess I am hungrier than I thought. Somehow I am already less self-conscious. Hank, Angelique, the flight attendant, the hip pilots and the dinner and drinks have at last put me at ease.

We eat in calm silence and then desert and coffee is wheeled out. I excuse myself and find my way to the tiny bathroom. There I fix my hair and touch up my makeup, and sigh at myself in the mirror as if to congratulate myself for finding such awesome new friends. I wonder where this will all lead. As I put my hands under the blow-dryer I feel proud of myself for taking a leap of faith. And it just proves that one never knows where life will lead you.

I'm ready for anything.

CHAPTER SIXTEEN

WILL

Yeah, Sylvia knows all about the incident at the bar between me and my college girlfriend. It was not what people perceived it to be on the surface. Nobody knew that I had conversations with my girlfriend and she had flat out said, "Please, tell me what you would do if you saw me flirting at a bar?" She was baiting me. Begging for retaliation. We wasted hours at night talking through various scenarios. We were mentally rehearsing for that moment in a way. We would lie in bed naked together and she would describe some made-up indiscretion. "Lets say I took up with a guy in one of my classes? There is a French exchange student who is really cute who just arrived this semester."

And I would take the bait. "What French guy?"

"He came to Grand Valley for the year. All the girls have crushes on him. I'm not saying that I do."

"Sure you do. You wouldn't have mentioned him if he had not made an impression on you."

She smiled like this conversation was heading exactly where she wanted it to.

"So lets say I, well I don't know, lets say I went out with him for coffee."

"I would not give two-shits."

"Okay, let's say I went to a movie with him? A French film with subtitles. You know how sensual French movies can be."

"Still wouldn't care."

"Okay, then lets say I spend the night at his dorm room but swore up and down that nothing happened. Would you believe me? Or would you get all hot-headed and rough me up a little?" she said, smiling.

After that nightly hypothetical chit-chat she finally went through with it. I found out from a friend of a friend. And I snapped.

What red-blooded American man wouldn't?

I'm not saying she wanted it. I'm not saying that she was asking for it. I'm not sure what I am saying. All I am saying is that she drove me crazy and I became physical with her and pulled her by her hair to the alley next to that collage bar. In my mind this was an act of love. A show of my devotion. Perhaps my urges came from deep inside my DNA and could be traced to the surely violent mating dance between a caveman and his cave woman. I am saying I acted like a primitive man. And I am admitting that I lost my mind that night as I did once again with my wife Sylvia, years later. Maybe I have always had a screw loose. A missing link. Maybe I had a subconscious propensity to repeat my patterns by choosing women that pushed my buttons and got under my skin.

Now, I watch you Sylvia, as you deboard that small luxury private plan with Hank and Angelique. And then when you take that private town car to the city, I am happy for you. And yet I am also seething. I am happy for you because you have always been a drifter of a woman. Drifting from man to man with no clear purpose. You always get your man. Because you light up a room with your smile. And because of your infectious laughter. Truly, I always felt you could have been a movie star. You are photogenic in your Instagram selfies. You put girls half your age to shame. No matter the angle of the shot. You always look to me like a throwback to the great stars of Italian Cinema. Fellini would have cast you in *La Dolce Vita* if he could.

Sylvia, I still love you. I love you from my dark matter to your active neutrons. I know that women find it intoxicating when a man falls deeply in love with them. And men try to avoid this state of heart and mind like the plague. Because being madly in love with a woman is one of the most dangerous and precarious states for a man to be in. It makes him vulnerable to the flipside which is the need for utter possession of her. In many ways I loved you so much that I actually wanted to be you. As I watch you in that town car on the highway to the city I must confess that when you were not home I would luxuriate in your closet. I would take in whiffs of your blouses, sweaters, leggings and your dresses. I would bury my face in your bra and panties and inhale your scent. Once when you weren't home, towards the end, when I was surely losing it, I stripped naked and put on your panties and bra. My cock protruded out on all sides of those thong panties. Your bras just barely fit around my chest. Then I flopped down in our bed and touched myself the way you must touch yourself. I tried to envision your female fantasies. I know this might sound sick. But I would think of myself the way you might think of me during out sexual acts. I imagined myself hovering over myself. And then I would further twist my twisted mind and dare to imagine another man, perhaps the giant-sized plumber who had recently come over our house and unclogged the drain in the bathroom sink. This circus freak-sized man's head almost touched the ceiling. His pants barely contained his beer belly and when he stooped under the sink to remove the pipe we had to contain ourselves when we witnessed his ass crack that looked like the cleavage of a buxom woman. And I knew, at least I thought I knew, that I bet you were speculating as to the size of this maintenance man's cock. His pungent aroma permeated the house. This was a sweaty hard working man stiff.

Now that was a specimen of an alpha male! And I just knew you wanted him inside you. And there I was in our bed dressed in your panties and bra pretending I was you and the plumber was on top of me.

How pathetic!

It was then that I had decided to seek help. And the next morning I sneakily contacted a psychiatric referral service and I scheduled an intake with a shrink. They asked if I had a preference for a male or a female doctor and I thought it was the safest bet for me to go with a man. They asked me to hold on the line while they went though their schedule to see who might be available the soonest. I was left listening to soothing new-age music on the phone line and then when the woman on the phone returned she said, "Hello again, Will. The soonest that we have a psychiatrist available for you is in two weeks. We can schedule you for a 9 a.m. appointment with Dr. Meadows."

"Perfect," I said.

CHAPTER SEVENTEEN

DR MEADOWS

This rarely happens when I feel that perhaps my initial evaluation of a patient might not have been conclusive. And that is the case when it comes to Sylvia Henderson. Now, of course to be transparent, I am fully aware my motives are not entirely professional and therapeutic. I am thinking this as I stand across the street from her home. I have her address on her phone bill which is in the pocket of my jacket. I am curious about this woman. I feel butterflies in my stomach. Yet actually, she is the butterfly that I have an itching to somehow capture. And contain.

This is not some sort of puppy love-at-first-sight that one might read about in a Hallmark Card. I am well-aware that I am a man of sixty-four – and a "happily" married man at that – with three grown children all doing remarkably well out in the big bad world. They no longer need me nor do they seek me out very often. What I am saying is that I can no longer run from the fact that under my cool demeanor is my growing need to somehow capture this woman's essence. And this simply never happens to me. I have had plenty of provocative women in my office who I sensed were attempting to subconsciously seduce me with their posture and the provocative things they shared. This is common in my practice. These women were clearly suffering from mild symptoms of nymphomania. None of these women phased me in the least.

But Sylvia is an entirely different sort of unconscious seductress. Or maybe I am just projecting. My plan is fairly simple and straightforward and it has been hand-written to myself with my Mont Blanc pen on legal paper in my other pocket.

Contact Sylvia Henderson. Request that she come to the office to retrieve her lost phone bill and discuss new breakthrough treatments that require only minimal doses of medication, coupled with half an hour of talk therapy, every two weeks.

I get back in my car and go back to the office. I wish to see her as often as I can, but I don't want to overwhelm or make her suspicious of my motives which are to isolate her like a specimen. Almost like keeping a brain in a jar. So that I can observe her. And of course, have her all to myself.

To be modern and up to the minute I text her in a manner that a pharmacy might text a client informing them their medication was ready for pick up.

Hello Sylvia,
This is Dr. Meadows and your phone bill must have slipped out of your purse. Text "Yes" if you are able to come to the office on Friday October 10th at 11 a.m. to retrieve it. We would not want your phone service to be discontinued.

I am simplifying my black widow trap by only asking her to confirm her attendance.

And isn't the word *"Yes"* what any smitten scientist of the mind desires to hear from the object of his new specimen of lethal femininity?

CHAPTER EIGHTEEN

SCOTT

I miss her. I honestly don't know why Sylvia suddenly leaves town. I don't understand why she is doing this. It doesn't feel right. Sylvia told me she has a business meeting in New York City with a VIP.

What business exactly is she in?

From what I know of her she is solely in the business of spending half the day in her PJs. Or perhaps she might take Sweetie for a couple of walks. Other than that she has never shown herself to be an ambitious woman. Besides those one or two Friday nights per month when she leads those night classes at her Paint and Sip. I don't want to press the issue. Up till now I have treated her with kid gloves like she is a veteran of Iraq who has seen combat. Look, I know all about what she did. And it doesn't scare me in the least. Her husband deserved to die like a dog. Mostly I am angry that in many ways, this beautiful woman that I love has been damaged.

I am working on a roof this afternoon. My "boys" are hammering away. And I am thinking about Sylvia. I am scared shitless that she will meet some high roller in Manhattan and give me the brush off. Or worse yet, simply ghost me.

The shingles that the homeowners have chosen for this roof are a putrid shade of green. I am finding myself to be repulsed by their color choice. But the homeowner is always right. They are not the first to chose this color which the boys and I call, "puke green."

The sun is blaring down on this unseasonably hot October afternoon. It must only be seventy-five degrees but it sure feels like ninety. There's no place to get relief from the sun when I'm working on a roof. Sometimes an extra-tall tree might provide shade but that is rare. I have forgotten to bring my water bottle and I am really wanting to drink from one of my buddy's water bottles. But we don't do that. Even roofers have protocol and boundaries. You simply never drink from you buddy's thermos.

My heart is beating fast and I am in a sweat. I am feeling a bit faint. I decide to tough it out and wait it for the feeling to pass. I sit down on the hot shingles. It feels hot as hell on my ass. I am getting it from above and below.

This is pure hell for me. Sylvia, I truly love you. It may be a simple and old-fashioned love. But it is genuine. You and me have been coasting along, with our thing, that we haven't even defined. We are one step further from just being friends with benefits. And so far that has been cool by me. But right now I'm not feeling very good.

Look, I am the World Series bingeing, fried chicken wings eating, drink you under the table, pass you on the highway, slap your ass when we fuck, kind of hard working guy. I *don't* faint like a pussy. It's not something that I do. But the thought of Sylvia leaving for New York City plus the heatwave has caught me totally off-guard and has knocked me off my game.

The blood feels like it is draining from my face. My

mind and my body are no longer mine. I'm the hot sun's bitch now. I feel my eyes roll in their sockets and then I find I am tumbling like a fireplace log down the angled slope of the roof of this two-story house. I have gone limp. Gravity pulls me off the edge and I land with a thud on some bushes, its branches cutting into my skin, and black out.

When I come to, I am in the gurney already. My guys are crowded around saying, "Scott man, you okay?"

But I cannot answer through the oxygen mask covering my face. I try to lift my hand and even that is tied down by an attachment to my finger which is monitoring my pulse. There is already an intravenous needle and a tube attached to my shoulder. I am grateful for the air-conditioning once I am in the ambulance. One of the EMTs is a hottie. She is calmly staring down at me. I guess she doesn't want to panic me.

"Just relax, Scott," she says. "Your vitals are stable and you didn't break anything. But we want to examine you and get some fluids in you as you are pretty dehydrated. You have a mild case of heatstroke. Just keep breathing, easy and slow."

She is a slim black woman with dreads in her hair. She wears bright green eyeshadow, which makes her look like a young woman at a rave. She smells good too.

Once they have wheeled me in my gurney into the ER department she rolls me down a few halls until we get to my new bed between curtains, then gently helps me get on the bed.

"How are you doing?" she asks, smiling.

"Much better with you around," I want to say. But I would never dare say such a thing. Her good looks and sweet compassion is working better than smelling salt would in snapping me out of my stupor.

A nurse enters. She is pretty with her frayed, dirty-blonde hair. I have always had good luck when it has come to nurses. Most of them have been lookers and that always helps. The nurse carefully attaches some wires to me.

The two of them exchange some technical talk that I can't decipher. Something about my heart rate. The nurse looks in my eyes and asks me my name and my address and then she asks me who is the president of the United States and I answer them correctly, except I tell them that the president is, "Kanye West." Just to bring a smile to their faces. And my EMT worker laughs.

"Okay, just lie back and relax, Scott," the nurse says. "Your ankle looks swollen so we're going to need to give you an X-ray. But other than that, you are one lucky guy."

My pretty EMT worker nods her head affirmatively.

By this time I'm high on whatever painkiller they plunged into my drip.

"I will be right back," the nurse says, leaving me alone with sexy EMT, who, combined with the drugs, is now the love of my life.

For the time being I have totally forgotten about my issues with Sylvia.

"Looks like you're going to make it," EMT says, touching my arm gently.

I feel goosebumps.

"Well, this is par-for-the-course in my line of work. Doesn't happen often but once in a while you hear about one of the guys taking a fall."

"You must have strong bones."

"The strongest."

"Your nurse is right. You just need to relax. And

they will have you out of here in no time at all."

Drunk with my drip I just blurt out, "Listen, what's your name?"

"Camellia," she says.

"Nice name. You have really been so good to me. You are gifted at what you do."

"We like to help people. It's just our job."

"I am only talking about you and nobody else."

"Well it takes a team to keep you safe."

"Any guy that gets in your ambulance surely falls for you."

"You're a funny one."

"No, listen, I am serious." I now am high as a junkie. "I'd like to know if there is a way I can reach you. To thank you. I mean shit, I fell off a fucking two-story roof."

"You're going to look back on what you say now and really feel embarrassed. You've been given strong pain relief. I'm just a person doing my job, Scott."

"I don't care if they have me on heroin. You need to know that I am dating a woman named Sylvia. it's a casual thing. But we have an understanding and things are cool. And now she goes off to New York City to do God knows what. It bugs me. And I have tried to be understanding and to show her that I accept her no matter what she does. And then I saw you. And I realized that maybe it isn't meant to be with Sylva and me. Give me this one chance to contact you once I am on my feet. We can do something simple and have coffee. Do you have somebody special in your life?"

"I am not at liberty to talk about my personal life. I don't think this is the time and the place. This is your time. We have to get you back on your feet."

"I would get on my feet right now and profess my

love for you if I wasn't hooked up to all these wires and a freaking catheter for all I know."

"Well, I'm sorry Scott, but I really think these are the pain-killers talking. I really have to go now. You are in good hands here. I have to get back to work. I suggest you work things out with your woman. That is always the best thing. A good woman like that is hard to find. You have to trust her while she's out of town. She's just doing whatever she has to do. We all are. Just give her some space and she will come right back to ya. I got my own things to work out with my man."

The nurse comes back in, takes me down for an X-ray and wheels me back to my room within half an hour. "Okay, Scott, we are going to wrap your ankle up. You can walk out of here with crutches. You might have to call an Uber."

"Can't I catch a ride back in the ambulance that brought me here with this lovely lady?"

Camellia gives my nurse a wink. "Okay, I gotta get back to work. Scott, remember what I said. And I do hope you are on your feet soon. And be careful up there on those roofs. Keep yourself hydrated so this doesn't happen again."

"Camellia, you have broken my heart."

I am so high on the ER's potions that I am truly making a fool of myself. And when I am intoxicated I know damn well that I get pushy. It has gotten me into plenty of trouble at parties. At bars it had brought on a few brawls. Right now I just have to suck it up and leave that poor girl alone. I am vaguely aware that what I am doing is nearing harassment.

They send me home with a bottle of codeine. I drop one. My drugged thoughts return to Sylvia. I text her and tell her what has happened to me and she still doesn't answer. I flop down in my bed and switch on the TV.

CHAPTER NINETEEN

SYLVIA

I can't believe it. Scott finally fell off one of those damn roofs! I have always thought it is a precarious and dangerous line of work that he is in. He texts me while I am at some fancy seafood restaurant midtown. I don't even know the name. But I do take note of the pricy menu. From what I can see nobody can leave the place without spending at least a hundred dollars. The ambiance is spectacular and dimly-lit by candelabras. Hank had asked me if I wanted to freshen during the flight. He told me that he planned for my visit to New York to take off with a bang as soon as we landed. So I showered and changed on his private jet. The bathroom shower was a bit cramped but as I showered I could look out a window in wonder at the sun and the sky which gave me the sensation that I was floating in the air.

Now I am dressed in a deep blue satin ensemble as we sit at a small round table. Just Hank and me. The waitstaff here are all male. We have ordered martinis and the gin has already taken me over. I excuse myself to text back to Scott that I wish him a speedy recovery. I do feel guilty for not being there for him. But I have to take this leap of faith with Hank. I need to get my life moving in a positive direction. I have been a possibly slovenly girl since the incident. Biding my time. Filled with survivor's guilt. Feeling like I have sinned against God and broken her sixth commandment: *Thou Shalt not kill.*

After texting Scott I excuse myself and use the restroom. The mirrors are tinted to compliment those who are want to feel good about themselves. My slinky one-piece plummets down to my navel like I am Cher in her early years. I look positively eatable. And I know it. Yet I wonder why I am doing this. Why must I attempt to be so alluring? I am not after Hank and from what I can see his intentions are strictly honorable.

Oh my, what do I really want? What am I doing to the men around me? Am I sending out mixed signals?

I return to sit with him at our table and I know I am doing it again with my smile and my intense gaze. On a few occasions when Scott has touched my hand as he speaks I have not pulled away. As I listen intently to him, I return the gesture and touch him back. After all, I feel grateful he has brought me to this five-star seafood restaurant. The waiter brings a towering tray with level after level of shrimp, mussels, oysters and sushi. If this really were our first date then I have no doubt somebody would be getting fucked tonight. And as my mind melts from the martinis and my mouth waters from the spicy clam sauce, I find that I am falling into a kind of trance. Hank is talking business. He is telling me that there might be some products I might want to endorse – perhaps home safety units or if I was willing, some feminine hygiene products. I haven't ever considered such things in my life before.

When I was married to Will I was mostly the glorified housewife. We considered ourselves liberated but the truth was I did the lioness's share of the cooking and cleaning while he put the bread on the table. I had to admit that I liked being taken care of, supported, fed, housed, fucked, adored, put on a pedestal, possessed by him, questioned as to my whereabouts during the day and even when I was on the receiving end of his ridiculous jealous wrath, it was something, it was action, it made me feel alive. I could feel my nerves go electric when he would yell at me, because I knew he was so wrong in his fantasies of the life he thought that I led on the sly. When the truth was I had simply had a manicure pedicure and had taken in a matinee of a Christmas movie starring The Rock because I admired his biceps. I guess I have always idolized a good 'ole iconic male persona.

Overpower me, smother me, expose yourself to me, love me, kiss me, treasure me, keep me, and slap my ass while you are at it.

All these thoughts wash through my intoxicated brain and I am just relieved that I don't have Will as a husband anymore. Because if he caught me in a New York restaurant like this with a handsome entrepreneur like Hank he would have knocked over this dinner table, dragged me out to the sidewalk by my dark black hair and given me what I deserved.

All that is over. I am free. He is dead and gone. What a great advantage it can be to kill somebody. For me, killing him has been a great big problem-solver.

"Whatever you want me to do, I will do," I say to Hank, over a desert that consists of a very small scoop of mouth-melting peach ice cream sprinkled with snow-like white chocolate.

I feel like such an easy girl. But I must consider my future. Sure, I have a substantial financial nest egg.

But I have heard stories of people running through their savings and winding up homeless. Here is my chance to move up in the world.

Hank gives his credit card to our waiter with such a sleight of hand you would think he is a magician. When his card is brought right back we get up to leave.

"I'd like to show you a good time. Do you like nightclubs," he asks.

"I have not been in one for years. But sure, yeah."

An Uber arrives and we head downtown to some trendy new club in Chelsea, housed in what used to be a meat packing warehouse.

The club is called *Rare*. And I wonder if that is referring to a steak. We arrive at the velvet ropes. When the muscle-bound bald bouncer – who is a ringer for Vin Diesel – sees Hank he lets us right through with a wink. He gives Hank two complimentary passes and some drink tickets.

We walk though the white, modern hallways until we enter the main part of the club where a DJ with a minimalist set up stands on a very small platform with two laptops. He has skeletal facial features. He wears a simple crew-cut white T shirt and jeans so torn you would think he had been attacked by a knife-welding psycho. He presses a headphone to one ear and his expression is concentrated like his gig is rocket science. The dancefloor is full. All the young, hot chicks dancing make me feel like I am chopped liver compared to them. Some hold their drinks and sip through a straw as they dance. Others embrace their male or female counterparts in such a way that you would think that they were either deeply in love with them or high as hell.

Probably both.

Hank leads me to the VIP section which is guarded

by a woman in a glittery tank top who looks like she is wearing warrior makeup and is about to go into battle. Hank says something flirty into her ear and she giggles like he has just proposed his plan to eat her out in the bathroom a little later.

We are seated on a plush black couch and there is a small round table in front. Our waitress arrives and leans down to ask for our order and her dress falls in such a way that I can see her entire naked body. Her breasts are tiny and pointed and she is wearing black panties which might just be more information than I need at this time.

"Would you like champagne again?" Hank asks me.

"Sure," I say feeling about as sexy as a tomboy who has just been playing softball with the lads. I sure thought I was dressed to the Ts until I stepped into the haute couture club.

I am expecting him to get all seductive. Instead he keeps it all strictly business. "So, I see we are on the same page. I will have my people draw up a contract overnight. In the meantime, let's celebrate."

He takes his wallet out from his jacket pocket and removes a small envelope.

"Tell me, Sylvia, would you be interested in having an especially good time tonight?"

I tell him, as best I can, over the bass-heavy music, that I am not sure what he is getting at.

"I am taking about Molly, dear," he says.

I am hip enough to know that he is referring to the street drug, ecstasy. I feel blood rush to my face at the thought of taking it.

"I'm not sure. I'll have to think about that."

"Trust me, this is the good shit. After the effects wear off you will sleep like a baby and wake up refreshed tomorrow."

"I'm not sure if I trust myself on it."

"I will be here with you and I will make sure you are one hundred percent safe."

"But you're going to take it as well."

"Yeah, but I drop Molly so often I have built up a resistance to it. All it does is make me relaxed and that's about it. Very relaxed."

"Well, I don't have a resistance to it. What if I have a bad trip?"

"That only happens on LSD. And I don't go for hallucinogens. I like to feel really good."

"Don't we all," I say, and it occurs to me that I have not felt "really good" in a long time. Not since I did what I did one year ago. I simply have not allowed joy to re-enter my life. Even when I am with Scott there is always a side of me that is withdrawn and solemn.

Is it possible to be crying while laughing at the same time? Because that describes me almost all the time.

He takes one of the orange candy colored pills out of the envelope and hands one to me.

"Trust me, Sylvia. I won't let anything bad happen to you."

I throw caution to the wind and place the pill on my tongue and show him it is there like a mental patient showing a nurse she is going to honestly swallow her meds. And then I wash it down with some sparkling champagne.

For a time, over the blare of the music, and under the strobe lights, we try a strained attempt at small talk. He is telling me he has mixed feelings about continuing to live in New York City. He says there is trash everywhere, homelessness is rampant and the Subway stinks of ammonia and piss. I tell him I am surprised he even rides the subway. He says he doesn't allow himself to fall for the trappings of being a multimillionaire. He says his obvious choice of simple Old Navy clothing should tell me everything I need to know about his true nature. Rather than broadcast his good fortune he much prefers blending in with the crowd.

"Some of us are more comfortable behind the scenes. That's me. However, I have this hunch that you will excel in front the camera's gaze."

"What makes you think that?" I say, batting my eyes comically like Betty Boop. I am suddenly feeling kind of kooky and playful.

"Because you are the new woman of the moment. Women these days are projecting themselves as badasses. Women are owning their power. I say, let women run this world. Men have run it into the ground. Pussy power!"

I am, for a moment, taken aback by his use of the P word. But then I cannot help but laugh right along with him.

"Really, I am just an average housewife that was pushed to the edge. I had to react in a nanosecond. It was live or die."

"Exactly, you are a woman who refused to be victimized. Very powerful stuff."

I am suddenly overcome by a slow rush of bodily sensations. I feel like a thousand electric ants are crawling across my skin. And then I have a head rush that makes it feel like I am a teenage girl high on hash at a grunge concert back in the 90s. And I feel for a moment I am fearful that I will tumble off my chair in this VIP room causing a scene. I really am not in the mood to be rushed to a New York City ER. This buzz is coming on fast and strong and the last thing I want is to spend it in a waiting room. I don't want to have to answer questions from a doctor under harsh fluorescent lights. I want to say here with Hank and all the beautiful people.

"I can see that you are what is known as bugging out," Hank says with a knowing smile. "I suggest you chill out and just allow it to happen. Don't fight the feeling."

I do as he says and I take some deep breaths, and now it happens – good feelings take me over. Suddenly this is exactly the techno song I want to hear and everyone around me are sheer perfection. There is nowhere else I would rather be. I can't sit still. I want to dance. And not necessarily with somebody. I want to be dancing with myself.

"I'm going to dance. You are welcome to join me. But if not, that is also okay," I say to Hank, as I get up from my seat and head for the dancefloor.

"I'm not much of a dancer," he says. "By all means knock yourself out."

I leave the VIP area and join the crowd. I walk into the sea of dancers and wind my way to the center of the dancefloor where I move like a woman in a self-actualizing ceremony at some self-help seminar. I am gesturing in every direction and clutching my heart and running my hands through my hair. I kick off my heels and dance barefoot like this is *Burning Man* and my feet are stomping on desert sand. I don't need anybody. Not Scott. Not Hank. I just need me.

Wild and wonderful me.

Right now, I don't give a damn about what my thirties have in store for me. My mind rewinds to the days when Will and I were passionately in love. We were sure that we didn't need anyone but us. We became homebodies we closed the shades, we turned off our phones, we turned on the TV, we huddled under my mother's comforter, we ordered in and stuffed ourselves with the junk food while in bed. And then when I needed just a little bit of space, to breathe, to wander, to just read books at a local bookstore, or to take in a matinee by myself, well, he just didn't understand. There's nothing worse than a man that does not believe you or trust you. How could he really love me if he truly thought I was capable of all the sordid things that he accused me of?

All my thoughts of love gone bad are washed away by a tidal wave of lust. Hot young guys surround me. At thirty, I feel like the older stateswoman. I feel a tad dizzy and light on my feet. The synthesizers in the song that plays are levitating me to the heavens. I feel as though I am going to just float away. I feel somebody take my hand like a child might take hold of the string of a helium balloon. Suddenly, I am pulled back down to earth.

It is Hank.

He confidently puts his other hand on my waist and his manly energy centers me. I now have somebody to focus my vision on.

"You're going to be okay, Sylvia. I'm here," he shouts into my ear over the music. I follow my tunnel vision to his gaze. "Come on," he says.

He leads me by the hand through the dancing, drinking, laughing bodies. He takes me, winding, through this seemingly endless club.

He turns to me and once again has to shout, "Lets go somewhere where we can talk. Does that sound good?"

"Sure," I say. "I'm game."

Before I know it we are exiting the club and the bald bouncer is wishing us a good night like we are very special people to him. We hop into an Uber. I watch the city outside my window. As some sexy hip-hop song comes on the radio. Now I want to just move to this metropolis. Oh to be a city girl and to shop till I drop, or sit in coffee shops, or maybe catch a Broadway Musical...

"I would like to invite you to my apartment," Hank says. "Is that alright, Sylvia?"

Hank sounds so formal. Like he might have me sign a sexual consent form before any hanky-panky. I guess a rich guy like him can never be too careful. One discontented woman could bring his whole empire crashing down. He would have to settle with her out of court for millions to avoid a trial. Yet, I am not that sort of woman. Certainly not tonight.

"Sounds wonderful," I say, also sounding horribly cordial like I'm Julie Andrews in *The Sound of Music*. So I correct myself and add, "Fuck yeah," which is more apropos to the way I am feeling.

The Uber pulls up at Hank's building in Union Square. And like a true gentleman he helps me out and we enter the lobby which is all marble with faux roman sculptures and a running fountain. Hank nods to the front desk and we go to the elevators. We walk through a small hallway and enter his vast loft.

"Nice digs," I say.

"I've lived here for a decade. I can't complain."

"I wish I had the guts to live in a big city. I live near my father. He's all I have left."

I am surprised at myself for sounding like such a downer while I am feeling such elation.

"You have me now. I'm going to look after you. I think we both need each other."

"How can you possibly need me? You are the man who has everything."

"You have heard that cliché, it's lonely at the top. Well, I assure you it's true. A man in my position doesn't know who to trust. Especially women. They only want me for one thing."

"And men only want me for one thing," I add, with a giggle.

I look out his living room wall-sized windows at

Union Square park at night. The trees, the building, the pedestrians, it is all so magical in that Manhattan way.

Now I find that I am in a hurry to see where this is all leading. I mean no man, and I do mean no man, invites me into their apartment just for chit-chat. And as I look at Hank, I can tell that he is well-built under his jacket and I find myself wondering what he looks like with his shirt off.

"Alexa, play Sade," he says.

And in a second a retro 80s beat is playing and Sade's *Smooth Operator* soon coos. And though this music is from before my time, I have heard this sultry song during the cool-down at end of our Zumba classes a the Y back home.

Now he says, "Alexa, dim the lights."

And like a set in *The Phantom of the Opera* the room gets darker. He walks to the coffee table in front of the couch and lights some candles and I know just where this is going and I find that my body is tingling with anticipation.

He goes to the bar, pops open some wine and then he slowly walks towards me with the drinks.

"Tell me Sylvia, are you in the mood to mix business with pleasure?"

"I'm not sure," I say taking the glass and sipping. I can feel the music caress my senses and in this light Hank looks like a dashing movie star playing the role of the millionaire. He seems to me like a combo of Zuckerberg and Jason Statham. Hank has that scruffy unshaven look of a proudly balding man that I am now finding totally irresistible.

"You say you are not sure?" he asks, with the compassion of a sex addict group leader who is seducing one of his newest members.

"Well, I am not exactly in my right mind."

"Are you saying you are too high to consent?"

"I bet a guy like you might be nervous about a woman turning on you. Accusing you. I bet you want a signed contract before you fuck a girl."

Now I am being crass. And I don't know why. The Molly makes me feel like such a little potty moth. He just doesn't get it. If he had a head on his shoulders then he would just take me into his arms and strip me down right now. Sometimes a girl just needs a man to take the lead. To show her his desire. I am in the mood to be dominated and put in my place. If I were seated in a movie theatre watching this scene I would sip my diet coke, pop some popcorn in my mouth and heckle the movie screen and scream, "Fuck her for God's sake!" And I am sure that many in the audience would cheer and clap.

For a moment I see flashes of Scott's earnest face in front of me. What am I doing? He loves me. But I am not sure if I feel the same way about him. I am not even sure how I feel about Hank. This has nothing to do with love. This has everything to do with wanting to feel protected and overwhelmed by a powerful man. My nipples are erect at the thought.

Hank moves in to kiss me, not on my lips but on my neck, like a metropolitan Dracula.

As he kisses me down my neck he reaches for the straps of my slinky once-piece and gently slips them off my shoulders so that it falls to my feet.

I shiver and feel doubly exposed as we stand in front of this wall-spanning window and I wonder if there is a voyeuristic creepy peeping Tom out there with a telescope watching and perhaps videoing all of this on their phone. I don't care anymore. Let all of Manhattan watch us. I want this and I want it bad.

His kisses move down my neck to my breast where he takes first one then the other into his mouth and then continues his puckered journey downward until he reaches my shaved pussy. He buries his mouth between my legs and the soft, wet sensation sends shivers through me. I am pulling at his shirt until I lift it off his body, exposing his rock star thin and hairless torso. He keeps his head between my legs insisting that I have an orgasm before the world rotates even one more inch. And standing there, I feel like he is praying to my womanhood like I am a Greek Goddess. The soft sensation of his tongue takes me over. I have reached nirvana.

He stands up and unbuckles his leather belt and removes his jeans. He takes me by the hand like he did at the club and we walk though his vast duplex loft. We pass abstract marble sculptures and splashy paintings and futuristic furniture to his spacious bedroom. Everything ultra chic. He leads me to the bed and I lie on top and wait for him.

CHAPTER TWENTY

DR MEADOWS

I finally am able to get ahold of Sylvia after forty-eight hours of waiting patiently for a reply. She calls me while I am in my office and she happens to catch me between patients which is not an easy thing to do since I am in high demand, as I am one of a handful of psychiatrists practicing in Grand Rapids. People wait months for an appointment with me. Virtually no patient is able to reach me by phone except for emergencies. But when I see her name pop up on my Caller ID you can bet you Freudian ass I pick up.

"Hello, Dr. Meadows, this is Sylvia. You texted me."

"Yes, Sylvia, how are you?"

"Well, right now I'm in New York City, having the time of my life."

"Okay, sounds good," I say matter-of-factly. After all I am not her friend or her relative. I am just her spurned psychiatrist. "Listen, I don't mean to disturb your vacation. Was this trip preplanned or was it a spontaneous decision?"

"Spur of the moment. I can hardly catch my breath from the excitement."

"I see . . ." I say, trying to cast some doubt on her good feelings. "Well, I just called because I found your phone bill. We don't want to have your phone cut off. And I was going over my notes. And I do believe that you might benefit from low doses of a very effective mood stabilizer. From the sound of your voice, you seem ever so slightly manic which naturally can feel euphoric and pleasurable for a time. The danger is in the flip-side – a depression which can sometimes prove to be debilitating."

"Look, I honestly don't know what you're talking about. I'm having a good time. And I don't need you to tell me otherwise. I don't care what kind of doctor you are."

I am taken aback by her frankness "I don't mean to intrude–"

"Well, you are intruding. I came to you for help. And I am the one who ultimately decides on my mental health and what goes into my body. You don't need to be soliciting your drugs to me. And by the way, there are a hell of a lot better drugs a girl like me can take that I am sure put your FDA approved shit to shame."

"May I ask you a question?"

"You are asking if you can ask? Be a man. If you have something to say just get on with it."

"Okay, Sylvia, you sound a bit anxious, are you depressed in any way?"

"I was doing just fine until you called me and made me doubt my own sanity."

"Look, Sylvia, I am not going to force you to take anything that you don't want to. That simply would not be ethical in my profession. Why don't we compromise. I do think I can help you. You have been through a trauma that would shatter a weaker woman. You are a very strong person, I am not insinuating that you are not. I just think that I can help you. Even a small amount of talk therapy with someone like myself who has expertise with trauma can be quite beneficial to someone who has experienced the things you have. When are you returning to Grand Rapids?"

"That's none of you business. And I don't need the phone bill, thank you. I auto-pay online."

I'm not surprised by her bullheadedness. Sylvia has always seemed spritely to me. She is not easy to persuade. Yet my thirst to simply be alone with her must be quenched.

She hangs up on me.

My heart sinks. I still won't accept no for an answer. And I begin to kid myself, to delude myself, that I am even doing all this to help her and not because I want to isolate her like a bodily cell, for observation.

For once, I have to think of myself. My life at home is adequate. My kids are well-behaved and my wife is sufficient in the to "till death do us part" department. But before I die. Correction. Before I wilt away into decrepit old age – where no woman will even bother to tell me off me like Sylvia has – I want to dissect her unique spirit and passion. Sylvia, without her knowledge, has just shown me some passion, even though it was in the form of anger. Negative attention is still attention. I know now that I have the power to get a rise out of that feisty, beautiful, young woman. And now I have to somehow run into Sylvia again. I want to collect her like a monarch butterfly for further inspection.

I will now carefully orchestrate the inevitable.

CHAPTER TWENTY-ONE

WILL

She has always been that way. Attracting men like bees to honey. And to think that for a time I had her all to myself.

Our wedding was really quite modest and yet it still haunts me. As an associate professor who had yet to get my tenure – as far as money goes – I didn't have two sticks to rub together. In other words, even though plenty of Dostoevsky-loving literate coeds had crushes on me – with my favorite elbow-patched tweed jacket – I was broke as shit.

Sylvia and me were shacking up in my apartment over in Heritage Hill. It was a creaky little place with periodically bursting pipes and chilly breezes that blew through the thin walls in the winter. But it did have a fireplace and somehow, with the help of my thick turtle-neck sweaters, we stayed warm. Sylvia liked to wear my clothing, you know "boyfriend clothes" or in this case "fiancé fleece."

So her parents – back when her mother was still vibrant and alive – offered to finance our wedding which would take place in the garage of Sylvia's family home. They cleared out the bicycles, tools, rakes and the lawn mower. They scrubbed out the oil spots on the cement floor. Then they threw down a carpet and brought in chairs, tables and balloons which made the whole thing feel more like a birthday bash for a thirteen-year-old girl than a wedding between their daughter and yours truly. Her mother made her trademark chicken and rice and placed it in a huge bowl next to the grape punch spiked with vodka, which turned out to be extremely potent. A few of my guy friends came and a few gal pals – some of which I had slept with once upon a time. Sylvia didn't know and didn't ask. She had invited her girl gang who were all pretty and fun to be around, but none looked as stunning as Sylvia looked that night. Her mother had sewn for her an all white gown that was flowing, yet tight at the waist and it offered – thanks to a push up bra – a view of her cleavage that made her look ready for Vogue. Nobody much cared what I was dressed in. I purchased my discount tux at a second-hand groom shop. I also wore a beer belly revealing cumber bun.

Sylvia had an artsy uncle who lived in Santa Fe and fancied himself to be an abstract painter and he made a living doing it. He officiated the wedding and his speech before our vows was filled with new age spirituality as he was a Zen Buddhist and he believed in the afterlife.

How right he turned out to be about the latter!

It was a raucous wedding. Tables were pushed away to make room for wild dancing. Everyone cheered when I slipped the garter belt off Sylvia's leg.

That night we spent at my apartment. We didn't even make love because she became sick from the punch and vomited numerous times. I also felt nauseous but managed to hold down the dinner. In the morning, she felt better and she showered, drank black coffee and turned to me and kissed me and apologized for disappointing me on our big night. Then we made love, tenderly, like two naked soulmates who planned to spend eternity together.

I tried to make that happen. But it backfired on me. I drove us to Chicago where we stayed in a modest hotel on the Magnificent Mile and we took in a play and had a nice steak dinner and spent the weekend thinking that the world was made of love and kisses and fucking and ordering room service and nothing else.

Only later did we learn that marriage was a complex institution. For one, it meant more than the trivialities of trying to decide whether to go out to eat for dinner or if Sylvia or I would cook.

I was not as talented as Sylvia was in the culinary department. She really had a flair in the kitchen. And she just naturally took on the traditional role of being a wife and she did it with great panache. While I put in my hours and taught my classes at the community college she would shop and keep the house in meticulous order. The two of us fell into our new roles so completely and yet something was lacking. And we both knew what that was. It can be put quite simply. What was missing was me climaxing inside of her with the abandon of a man who wishes to get his wife pregnant. What was missing was the kind of lovemaking that was geared towards creating life rather than just getting off. Sylvia was not able to be on the pill because it threw her whole system off. It gave her headaches and made her breasts sore. So much so that she would not want me to kiss or to touch them. This proved detrimental for both of us. So we decided that I would wear condoms. Always. And this was not only pricey but cumbersome and took away the inherent spontaneity of early marital sexual bliss. First, we would engage in free-flowing foreplay and then would come the moment when she would say, "Put one on." And then I would fumble with the drawer in the cabinet next to the bed, rip open the package and slip it on. Of course this diminished the raw pleasure of feeling the soft, wet inside of my wife's pussy. All I felt was the constricting condom and my nostrils filled with the scent of latex.

I wanted a child. A boy to be perfectly honest. I wanted to teach him all about my love of poetry. I didn't want a sports loving, or baseball batterer, or grimy hulk of a football player. I wanted to bring up the sort of boy that might ace a spelling bee, or write an essay about the fallacy that Christopher Columbus discovered America and point out that indigenous people were the true explorers. And so on.

Yet, Sylvia made it clear that she wasn't ready to be a mother. And I saw that as selfish. I took it as an affront to my very genes and DNA. What greater compliment can a woman give a man than to want to give him a child that might just look, think, and talk like him?

And that was the beginning of the end of us. Or should I say the beginning of the end for me. I just didn't approve of my wife being such the social butterfly. Spin class, drinks with the girls. Coffee with Emma, the Zoo with Deb, shopping at the mall with Zoe. Soon she was forgetting to have my meal ready for me when I got home. And I didn't like that. Not one bit.

Look, it mattered that my dinner wasn't ready. If that made me a chauvinist, so be it. I just wanted her at home. I hated to come back from the university to an empty house. At first I didn't say anything about it. Instead, I kindled some friendships of my own. Namely with Sophia, who was a senior at the college.

It started when I invited her out for coffee at the Starbucks down the way from the college. She was a green-eyed and auburn-haired girl with heaving breasts that her thick sweaters could not conceal or contain. Yet she always kept them covered as she seemed intent on being loved for her preciously knowledgeable mind rather than her sumptuous body. It did not take me long to burrow past her boundaries.

All I really needed to do was wholeheartedly agree with her when she spoke ravenously about the – in my opinion – overblown writing of Thomas Wolfe. All I had to do was nod in approval when she recited works by Emily Dickinson. Even though I found it closeted and claustrophobic.

Next thing I knew, she was inviting me to see her book collection at the house she shared with an elderly woman who was mostly bed-ridden with a live-in nurse. Upstairs is where Sophia had her tiny incense-scented room with little ventilation. Yet it was cozy and cluttered with books and it didn't take long for me to make my professorial move and to take off my glasses and then gently reach to take off *her* glasses and go in for our first kiss.

Her lips felt wet, fresh and tasted like the strawberries of fleeting summertime. She was all but twenty-one and I was thirty seven at the time and that's what made it so damn sexy, immediate and oh-so-necessary. I was risking both my marriage and my tenure at the university. Yet I dared to kiss her behind her ears, and let her red hair cover my face. My main goal in life at that moment was relegated to simply getting that fluffy white wool sweater off of her. I reached for it and started to peel it off. By keeping her eyes closed she was allowing it all. I felt like I was opening a Christmas gift at the Playboy mansion. And what gifts she had!

Her breasts were like swooping white sand dunes and they were warm and inviting. I burrowed myself between her breasts as if it were there that I would find sexual salvation. As if it was there that death could never find me. As if it were there where I could hide from the riggers of my already failing marriage. It was the one place where Sylvia could never find me. I was alone with this young woman and her body and I felt fucking alive again. When she sighed the words, "please" and "yes" it triggered in me a sexual aggression I had waited so long to show. She willingly laid back in her bed of quilted comforters as outside the snow fell.

It was the December of my discontent.

I must have kissed every single part of her. And she did the same in return. In her case, I felt like she was searching my body for one ounce of common decency. I was horny, yet ashamed. I was indulging in the guilty pleasure and the undeniable honor of fucking a coed in the afternoon during the fall semester.

The rhythm of our bodies made her old bed creak.

Then she whispered a joke into my ear that really set me off. "Are you going to give me an A plus for fucking you?"

I didn't last long after that quip. This was far too much stimulation for a married professor of English. I gasped so loud during my orgasm that I feared the old crone downstairs might have heard me and was about to call the cops.

Sensing this Sophia said, "Don't worry she's almost deaf."

And the thought of a shriveled woman downstairs as I had this hot babe in my arms upstairs caught me off-guard, and I rolled over and sat up and announced that I had better get going. No post-coital conversation. No cuddling. No promises. No pillow talk.

"Really? You have to go?" she asked, gripping the comforter.

"Yes, I do. My wife is probably making dinner. We must be careful."

"Understood," she said, looking for and then finding her thick-lensed glasses.

When I returned home to my attic study where I graded my students papers I thought about her off-the-cuff joke. It stuck in my craw. She was right. I was the gatekeeper to her academic future. It was really just a cliché sex joke. But it hit home. How should I grade her now? She was a B minus student at best. Though she did excel in her essay writing skills. Yet, there was a hidden threat there too, wasn't there? Should I give her the grade she truly deserved I risked her immature retaliation. Upon seeing the mediocre grade she could easily go through with telling the faculty all about us. She was truly the one with the power. The power to utterly destroy my life. I was such a fool. I decided then and there that I would not jeopardize my pending tenure. I would give her an A plus and also immediately cut off all our trysts. I had to be strategic.

Sylvia, you were the one who brought on all this confusion when you didn't want to have my baby. Why didn't you want to? You made me do it. You made me do everything. And then you shot me dead.

Bitch!

CHAPTER TWENTY-TWO

HANK

I see a refreshing innocence in Sylvia. She hasn't been spoiled by her blood-stained past. And I believe the pubic will see this in her. What I didn't expect is that I would fall for her so completely, so quickly. At first I only saw in her dollar signs and a raw, unassuming charisma. Now I see that Sylvia has a mystery about her that just doesn't fit in with the sleepy city where she is from. I don't believe she belongs there. I think that living there is only going to burry her star quality in a cascade of winter snow. She needs to be on the East Coast. I plan to take her to some cocktail parties to see how my unit of PR agents, talent scouts, CEOs and money managers might feel about her. So in the morning, after we both wake at noon, we forgo making love again so that I bring her to a brunch Angelique has prescheduled.

I already sense that my assistant envies my interest in Sylvia in an unnecessary catty way.

We arrive at the popular midtown restaurant. It features a towering twenty-five foot ceiling and a menu where you can't even get eggs over easy for less than seventy bucks. Their eggs Benedict is to die for. I suggest it to Sylvia, touching her soft hair as I do. I am not about to hide our budding romance from my business partners.

Seated around the table are two twenty-something PR guys, one executive director of advertising, and two forty-something magazine gals who are always on the lookout for the next hot thing and know it when they see it. They eye Sylvia like two pansexuals considering a threesome. These are the wolves of the media industry and Sylvia is the rare meat.

"So everyone, this is Sylvia. My protégé. I believe she can endorse everything from a gym membership to a gun dealership. She could even be a brand ambassador for an insurance company or a line of Jeeps. She has amazing untapped appeal."

"Please, you're embarrassing me," Sylvia says, fanning herself with her cloth napkin like a geisha.

"No need to be modest with us," Lorna from Cosmo says. "This is your time to shine."

"Well, I don't want to disappoint you all. It seems you have such lofty expectations of me. And really I'm just your average former housewife."

"Not so average from what we hear," Lorna says. "Not many women would have the courage you had."

"Look, I don't want to only be known for one thing. I am not a one-trick pony. I'm a human being."

"You are a very attractive woman," my bald, thick-necked CEO friend says.

"Yeah I guess people don't expect a woman to kill her husband," Sylvia says. "But it happens all the time. Women fight back against domestic violence. And none of them get any credit for the pain they escaped. I don't know why everybody takes such an interest in what I did. And I wish there was a way I could have acted differently. Maybe I could have just grabbed my phone, run and called 911. I don't know.

It didn't help that I was stark naked when it happened. That can make one feel pretty vulnerable."

"You know something, let's give this whole subject a rest and enjoy our mimosas. We can talk about this at a later time," I suggest.

Sylvia seems pleased that I am standing up for her. I sense she feels protected by my presence. I have only her best interest in mind. These associates – who I have worked with for years – are looking for a piece of the pie. But I have found that in this industry that is the norm. Everybody wants a cut of a good thing. And there are simply not that many slices to go around, considering my plan is to take forty percent of Sylvia's earnings. I have not broken it to Sylvia yet that this is my desired percentage rate. Let me first entice her with a lucrative deal. When she sees all the zeros on the contract she will be more agreeable.

For the rest of our meal we all make New York City-styled small talk. They ask if she has taken in any shows yet. She tells them she has only been here for twenty four hours. And that is when I take my cue to signal the waitress and pay the tab and decide to whisk Sylvia away from all those inquisitive eyes.

Once outside I say, "I just had to get you out of there. Let's just have fun."

I take her to the Met where she confesses to me that she finds Greek and Roman statues of men with their chipped penises to be ridiculously hot. She cries in the van Gogh room. "What a sad life he led. And such a genius," she says. "What he needed was somebody like you to sell his art."

"He had his brother, Theo," I say.

"Yes," she says wiping her tears. "At least he had him. And I have you."

"Yes, you have me now, Sylvia."

Then we head back downtown and stroll around

the East Village where I take her to a quaint little French Bistro between First and Second Avenue. As we sip wine and wait for our food, Sylvia keeps checking her phone messages. She seems preoccupied. Like I am no longer there.

"Are you okay?" I ask her.

"It's nothing, really."

"Please, if you feel so inclined, tell me what is going on. I want to make sure this is a pleasurable vacation for you. But if it is a private matter I will understand."

"It is very private." She takes a sip of wine. "But you know something, I don't mind telling you. I just got a message from a doctor. Actually a psychiatrist. I was feeling a little funny for a while so my dad booked me an appointment. I was not into it but since my dad took the trouble to book it I decided to give it a try. During the consultation I told the psychiatrist that I was perfectly fine and didn't need medication. Then I picked up on some weird vibes from him."

"What kind of weird vibes?" I ask.

"I could not put my finger on it. But something was odd about him. Anyway, I told him I didn't want to schedule any further appointments and now he leaves a message for me claiming to have re-evaluated me and that he thinks I would benefit from medication and seeing him again. Something about this Dr. Meadows guy rubs me the wrong way. I just don't want to be psychoanalyzed, period. I know I am fucked up. From what happened to me, who wouldn't be?"

"Listen, Sylvia, it is your mind and body and it is ultimately your choice what you put in it. Some of those doctors are just drug dispensing quacks. Once you step into their little chemical world you can never escape because you become dependent on their shit."

"What should I tell him? He is a medical professional. I mean you should have seen all the framed certificates on his wall. Maybe he's right."

"I don't think so. You are the most dynamic, beautiful and well-adjusted woman I have ever met. Just call him back and say thanks but no thanks. Or better yet, don't bother. You owe him nothing."

"But then again what if I could benefit from some therapy?"

"I will let you know if I think you need any of that. I care about you. I didn't expect that what transpired between us would happen. It certainly wasn't my plan. I don't go around sleeping with my future clients. That's not my style. But there is something special about you. You are a survivor and I love that about you."

It is only now that I realize my words have just revealed far too much. I have thrown down all my emotional cards far too soon. I sense now that my saying the word "love" to her has quite possibly triggered something deep within her when she asks:

"Did I just hear you right?"

I hesitate to reply, taking in the ambiance of the Bistro. It is an understated, romantic place. Is the atmosphere and the wine making me reveal my feelings to her?

"Yes. I think after what we shared last night that it is safe to say I feel very strongly about you."

She inhales. Closes her eyes. "I'm flattered. And I'm not juts saying this but I too feel very passionately about you."

We fall into an unrestrained kiss right there in the café. We don't realize our pretty French server is waiting on us until she asks if we'd like anything else to eat or drink. I wonder how long she has been standing there while Sylvia and I have been lost in each other's mouths.

I move away, reluctantly, from Sylva and say, "I think we will have some coffee and whatever desert you have on special."

"The crème brulé it is"

When the desert arrives, we both take small forkfuls in silence.

I fear that when I present her with my slightly one-sided contract Sylvia will think I am trying to take advantage of her Midwest naïveté.

I invited her here to make a business proposition. Yet this has unexpectedly blossomed into something more.

CHAPTER TWENTY-THREE

SCOTT

Sylvia comes back from her New York City visit today. I have the keys to her house as I have been watching her dog. And I have decided to tidy up a little. As I am mopping her kitchen, for the first time, I convince myself – though the flooring has been replaced – that I can see the bloodstains from her late husband. Nevertheless, sometimes I can feel the presence of her husband. She really shouldn't have remained living in this house. She really should sell it and move to another part of town. But then again, the property is tainted. People talk. And I imagine it would be almost impossible to sell a home where a fatal shooting has taken place.

I have done some innocent snooping around. She certainly doesn't keep a diary. I am just wondering if she shows interest in others as I did at the ER. But I attribute that mostly to the analgesic drip. From what I already know about Sylvia, she leads a fairly organized and impressively clean life. Yet there is something static about this place. I see numerous framed pictures in her bedroom of her deceased mother. There are photos of her mother in her youth. Anne was a striking woman in her time. Mother and daughter share many features – the full lips, and the thin, mostly penciled-in eyebrows. Her mother was also a brunette with a sultry figure, with that infectious smile. I lean into one of the photos of her mother. So close that for a moment I feel like I can feel the very breath of her exhalation. I am startled by this sensation and I step back. Her mother's eyes seem to look at me from within the frame. Like she is watching to make sure I take good care of her daughter. I have never been a believer in ghosts but if any house has ever felt haunted this one certainly does.

There are no photos of Sylvia's husband, Will. I fully understand why. All those photos – that is if she has not deleted them – would most likely be on her phone.

Her mother was of another time.

It feels like all of the faces in the photographs are staring at me. Watching me. If I didn't think it would be totally out of line, I would take all the photos and stash them in the recesses of a dark, musty closet.

Though I've no doubt Sylvia would kill me if I did such a thing.

CHAPTER TWENTY-FOUR

SYLVIA

As I fly alone in Hank's private jet back home to Grand Rapids I am not sure what to do with all the exhilaration I feel. I have been stimulated from head to toe. I have tasted culinary delights from the finest restaurants in the city. At the Metropolitan Museum of Art I stood before the melancholy last self-portraits painted by Rembrandt and the festive, decorative brushstrokes of Matisse. I have felt the earthy sun-soaked phallic powers of the totem poles of ancient Africa. And I have been fucked raw in Hank's multi-million dollar duplex in Union Square. I can barely walk with my legs together. And now I have to go back to my hard-working boyfriend, Scott, who has been house and dog-sitting for me. I am sure he will be as eager as Sweetie to see me. But now the excitement has worn off, I am seeing things a little differently.

Hank calculatingly seduced me with luxury, compliments, culinary delights, drinks and drugs. While Scott earnestly tries to prove to me that he is nothing like my late husband. Yet, I am not beholden to either of these men. My loyalty is to myself.

As I step out of that small aircraft I can only hope

that Scott won't instantly suspect I have betrayed him. Will he pick up on Hank's scent? I showered and scrubbed myself vigorously at Hank's loft. Yet sexual guilt is hard to wash off. If Scott dares to question me I'm not sure what I will say. How I will be able to look him in the eye.

As I walk though the tiny airport rolling my carry-on behind me, I both look forward to and dread seeing my faithful and so very kind boyfriend.

And there he is. I spot Scott standing beside his idling, muddy Jeep. He is dressed in cowboy boots, jeans and a lived-in leather jacket.

We embrace beneath the stars and I can feel his physical strength. He has the power to squeeze me to death.

As he drives me home I wonder if perhaps I was meant to die one year ago. Am I now courting death again by cheating on such a virile man? In the past we have gone to some bars. And he has had a couple too many drinks and I have seen him get into some altercations. I have never seen him in action. Yet, I'm sure those bulging biceps of his can do some serious damage. You don't fuck around with a guy like Scott. I have seen him with his co-workers – who he calls his "boys". If they mess up he shouts, "Fucking get on the ball or I am going to push you off this fucking roof!"

They laugh it off like it is just banter, but I know that if push comes to shove, he'll shove.

And yet as I walk into the door of my home I bare witness to the side of him he shows to me. My house is adorned in rose pedals. Soft acoustic guitar music plays on the speakers in my living room. All the lights are dimmed. On my dining room table is a bowl full of Hershey's kisses, two bottles of red wine and one pre-rolled joint.

"What is all this about?" I ask.

"It's about you. It's about you and me. It's about how much I have missed you. I know I have never been much good at the whole romantic Hallmark card sort of thing. And I think maybe I have been taking you for granted, working so hard lately. So I thought I would do something special for you."

"How did you think of this?" I ask, because I am damn sure he didn't come up with this idea on his own. Maybe he cheated like I did and feels guilty.

"Well, to be honest, I just googled the phrase "romantic evening." And one of the first things on a list was to throw rose petals all around the place. Do you like what I've done?"

"Of course I do. Were you worried I wouldn't?" I ask.

I am the one who is tense and projecting my anxiety on him.

"I just wasn't sure how you would react. I was going to put candles everywhere and light them and then you could come back to candlelight. But then I thought it might be a fire hazard and I don't think you would be too happy if you came home to find out I had burned your house down."

"Smart move."

Sweetie waddles into the living room. I pick her up and allow her to lick my face in greeting.

"Its good to be home," I say, setting her down again.

I had an amazing time yet I am still not convinced about big city living. Something about Manhattan makes me uneasy. It's busy and noisy and after a while I just wanted some peace and quiet.

Scott walks over to the wine on the dining room table. "Shall we?"

"Sure," I say, even though I have been through an intoxicating-enough weekend high on weed and

Molly, and drunk on champagne, martinis and mimosas. There is a part of me that longs to be sober. So that I can think things through. Yet, I know that Scott has his own needs. He wants me. And I know exactly what he wants.

After two glasses of wine he waits for me to invite him upstairs to my bedroom. I'm sitting on the couch with Sweetie on my lap separating us.

"I hope you don't mind," I say to him, while petting Sweetie. "But I think I'll have an early night."

"Oh, okay. I understand. Can I still . . .?"

"Still what?"

"Spend the night here?"

"Sure," I say. "But no hanky-panky."

"Cross my heart and hope to die," he says.

He follows me upstairs like a spurned sex slave. He gets in my bed and with the remote switches on the TV while I undress, and it occurs to me that this is the first time I have ever withheld sex from Scott. And then I get a flashback to when I did the same to Will. And how he didn't exactly take it too well. My husband had gone hog wild. He became a madman who simply could not function. Seeing that scared me, which inevitably led to my withdrawal from him.

Why am I doing it now?

As I put on my PJs I come to the conclusion that my life is spiraling in directions I could never have anticipated. When I close the door of the closet Scott is standing there.

"Boo!" he jokes.

"Come on, you really freaked me out," I say.

"Just thought I would have a little fun."

"I don't find it funny."

"Sorry, I was just trying to bring a smile to your face. You seem grumpy."

Sweetie slowly steps into the room. I help her up

onto the bed and place her on its center where she loves to sleep nightly.

"Is it okay if I undress too? Or do you want me to sleep in my jeans?" Scott asks, sarcastically.

"You can sleep any way you like."

We get in bed. The news is on.

"Is it okay if we cuddle?" Scott asks

"I suppose," I say, relenting to this new cutesy act he is putting on. I know what is underneath it all. And that is a man who is hungry to take me into his arms and have his way with me. I scoot Sweetie down to the foot of the bed so that Scott and I can cuddle.

"I'm sorry to be this way," I say, as he wraps his legs around mine and snuggles his face into my neck.

"It's okay."

He begins to kiss my earlobe.

"Please don't," I insist.

"Why not? Is your earlobe off limits too?"

"It's not that."

"What is it then?"

"Can we talk about this tomorrow? I'm tired."

"Tired of me?"

"No."

"Then what are you tired of?"

"I'm just tired. Is that quite alright with you!?" I pull away to my side of the bed.

If turning me on is his goal, his persistence is having the opposite effect on me. There is a part of me that wishes he *would* go home. I need my own space.

"Okay, I accept that you are tired. But tell me this," he sits up in bed, his firm, hairy chest illuminated by the flicker of the TV screen, "you go to New York to check out a career opportunity and you come back distant and waspish – why? I'll understand if you're on the rag."

"Please don't say 'on the rag' thank you."

"Okay, when it is that time of the month. But other than that, well, it's just not cool," he says.

"I think you are making too big a deal of this."

And then in a sudden fury of movement, Scott gets up out of bed and begins searching for his shirt, jeans and boots.

"What are you doing?"

"Going home. It seems to me you just want to be alone."

"Please don't," I say. Though there is a part of me that thinks he should.

"No, really. It's totally cool," he says, snapping on his belt.

I just sit and watch him go. I hear the front door slam and then the sound of Scott's Jeep starting up. And now I take hold of Sweetie and pet her and I say, "I am in such a fucking mess!"

I have a restful night's sleep, despite the thoughts whirring around inside my head.

In the morning, I awake to the sound of my doorbell. I hop out of bed, slip into my slippers, throw on my bathrobe and head downstairs, as I pass the clock on the wall.

10 a.m.

Who could be calling at this ungodly hour?

CHAPTER TWENTY-FIVE

DR MEADOWS

Sylvia stands before me. I take her in with one glance with her pencil-thin eyebrows, and her sleepy brown eyes, dressed in PJs and a bathrobe. Her bare feet reveal pink-painted toenails.

"Hello, Sylvia," I say. "I hope I'm not being intrusive. I just happened to be in your area and I thought I would stop by as opposed to leaving another text or voicemail."

"Yes, I got your message and was meaning to get back to you." She looks ever-so-slightly annoyed. "How do you even know where I live?"

I am sure now she knows that psychiatrists are not usually in the practice of making house calls.

"Well, I thought we could talk for a moment. If this is a bad time I will totally understand. And to answer your question. I got your address from your phone bill." I take it out of my pocket and extend my hand.

Sylvia looks left and right as if there were somebody else home which I sense there is not. Then she looks down at her own morning attire.

"Well, I have not even had my morning cup of coffee. Can this wait?"

"So you don't want your phone bill?"

She quickly snatches it from my hand.

"Yes, absolutely it can wait. But the sooner I relay this information to you the better. For your sake."

"For my sake? You make this sound like a medical emergency."

"We could talk here or you could . . ." I pause and then in my least threatening tone say, "invite me in for a cup of coffee."

She takes in my words. I can tell that she feels uncomfortable by the way her toes curl.

"Look, I'm not a morning person. Can you just give me a hint as to what this is all about. I know you told me in a text but I hardly had time to read it."

"I would prefer to schedule another appointment with you so we can talk about it in my office."

"Let me think on that. Look, I feel perfectly fine. I mean I just got back from having a crazy good time."

"Crazy good?" I say mirroring her words back to her as a way of creating an artificial sense of my being on her level.

"Yup."

"How did you sleep?"

"I hardly slept."

"Sleep is very important for . . . sensitive minds with . . . certain dispositions."

"What are you hinting at?"

"I think you would benefit from–"

I read that part of your message. You want to get me on drugs."

"Medication might be a better word for it." If I can only sedate her. Then I could see her being perfectly still. Study her. Examine her. Maybe even caress her.

"I like being me. I don't want to be numb. I want the full gamut of my emotions. Especially now. Dr. Meadows, I am having the time of my life. And I am not seeking your services. And I seriously doubt it is part of your code of conduct to be coming here to solicit. So for now, I am going to treat you like any door-to-door salesman and say thanks but sorry, I'm not interested."

Sylvia practically slams her front door on my nose. Yet, I am not phased. I know I have gotten under her skin. And I could tell from our first meeting that she doesn't trust me. So I will have to reach her in some other way. Perhaps if I abandon the professional stance and appeal to her on a personal level, as a friend?

As I start up my car, I see her peeking through the front curtains of her window. It is then I know that I might have to take matters into my own hands. I may as well drop all pretension. I have already stepped out of the norm and showed up at her house. If she were to report this to my associates just this alone might strip me of my license to practice.

As I drive through the upscale neighborhood streets, I switch on the radio and try to quell my thoughts. I am mulling over what is mine. My wife, my children, my practice. And I realize that my life can be portioned into ten or twenty-minute intervals. That is about how long I spend on those who come into my office for a script. And then I spend roughly twenty minutes having dinner with my wife before I spend twenty minutes reading *The Wall Street Journal*. I prefer it to cable news. I am old-fashioned that way. And then when I go upstairs I spend twenty minutes in the shower and about twenty minutes in bed with my wife of twenty years. The performance takes all of twenty minutes. I know that to be true because often, when we are in our standard missionary position and I am facing our digital clock, it has always been a habit of mine to time my diminishing virility.

Tonight my wife lies naked under me. I picture Sylvia as we kiss. I close my eyes and I can see Sylvia's big brown eyes and the danger they convey. Sylvia's duality fascinates me. She is both fragile and deadly. I have this fantasy of her placing a loaded gun to my temple as I fuck her.

My wife grabs me by my chin and forces me to look into her eyes as we copulate. I do as she wants yet I am only pretending to connect with her.

Once sated, she drifts off to sleep, while I lie there staring at the shadow-play on the ceiling. I imagine myself dissecting Sylvia's psyche.

Her blood-stained physiological mysteries beckon me.

CHAPTER TWENTY-SIX

WILL

Thank God Sylvia put that Dr. Meadows creep in his place. Kudos to her. That sonofabitch is no more than a government sponsored drug dealer.

Now she calls her trusted confidant – her dad.

Harold and I used to pal around. We had a simpatico rapport. From up here I watched his reaction when he found out I tried to kill his daughter. And that she shot me dead. He was heartbroken and cursed the day he'd welcomed me into his home.

They used to serve me hearty meals, he and his wife, when Sylvia took me for weekends by Saugatuck to spend time at their lake house. We would go for walks in the summer and share our love of 20th century literature. Sylvia's dad once told me that in his youth he had fooled around with fiction writing but found he didn't have the necessary diligence. He was a family man. Sylvia was their only child. He bought her first apartment. Then came Sylvia's short marriage which was harmless enough. Just a youthful mistake. They lasted about a minute.

And then she met yours truly – the worst thing that ever happened to her – and we bought the house where she now lives. The most erroneous choice she ever made.

I watch her as the two of them meet for another one of their weekly lunches. This time they go to the pricy place on Reeds Lake called *Roses*. It is already too chilly to sit outside.

"Dad, I am confused," she says, while looking over the menu.

"Man trouble?"

He is right. She sure can pick 'em.

"I met somebody. His name's Hank. You'll like him."

"Now hold on a minute, what about your roofer guy?"

"We aren't exclusive."

"What about this new guy?"

"He wants to sign me."

"Sign you?"

"Yes, he thinks that because of my history I could be branded and used to help sell things."

"Wouldn't that put you in the public eye? Something you wanted to avoid not so long ago? And what about Scott? I thought you liked him? You should think this through."

"That's why I'm telling you. I have a decision to make and I don't yet know what to choose."

"How much is this Hank guy worth?"

"Millions."

"So he's not after your money."

"No, dad."

"I see. Well, Scott is a paycheck to paycheck sort of dude and so I can see the appeal. How long have you known Hank? I mean, he's whisked you away on a trip, offered you work and now you're what – in a relationship with him? And I'm only just hearing his name. Don't you think you're moving too fast? I can't tell you what to do. All I can say is be careful. You're a little too quick to judge and look where it got you? Take your time to get to know this man before you take things further. You're still young. You have plenty of time to fall in love."

Their meals arrive. I watch them eat it. Outside it is overcast and rain begins to sprinkle against the window. The lake looks dark. Soon it will be frozen.

After their lunch, Sylvia hugs her father goodbye. Sometimes, I was suspicious of their closeness. I never had that.

She drives home with the radio blasting as though she hasn't a care in the world.

I curse and kiss her from afar.

CHAPTER TWENTY-EIGHT

HANK

I have spoken to my people and they have spoken to their people and it is unanimous – we are bewitched by Sylvia. I am convinced that her market is mostly millennial women who see her as a hero of survivalism and feminism all wrapped into one sexy package. I am in touch with a perfume company working on a new, more robust scent for women. I know instinctively that this is our ticket.

I call Sylvia about it and she says she is agreeable to doing a screen-test. She tells me she is not much of a perfume enthusiast. She says she doesn't even go for scented candles or incense. She tells me she prefers unadorned human pheromones. She shares that back in high school she had a scruffy motorcycle riding boyfriend that hardly ever showered even after basketball games in the park. She found his sweat to be an aphrodisiac. She even goes as far as to tell me that she adores my natural scent in the morning and that I should stop using my expensive cologne. She says that all the masking of natural scents is what confuses the dating game which she considers to be quite primal in nature. I find her enchanting no matter how outlandish her ideas are. I remind myself that she has warned me that she is seeing a guy named Scott in her hometown. I want her for myself. I wish I could get her to sign an exclusive and binding contract to my heart. I need to see her again and I tell her so while I have her on the phone.

"Why don't you fly out this weekend?" I suggest.

There is silence on the other end of the line. Then she says, "That does sound tempting. But I need time to catch my breath."

I get off the line proud of myself for who I am now. I did some bad stuff in the past. Before I channeled all that misguided energy into my company. None of it is on my record because I did it before I became of age. Let's just say I had – and that is past tense – a nasty temper. And if you got on the wrong side of me you would have faced my wrath. There are a couple of guys in school that don't remember me so fondly and I am lucky they don't threaten to come forward to the press about me. If they did I would just have to buy their silence. My public image cannot afford it.

I was at my worst high or drunk. And so maybe I can relate to Sylvia's dead husband, Will, in some ways. I could have easily been that guy that squeezes a little too tight during rough sex with a woman who'd done me wrong. Look, I have changed. I never did then and I never would lay a hand on a woman.

Or in one particular case a switchblade.

CHAPTER TWENTY-NINE

SYLVIA

I sign Hank's contract after consulting a lawyer. My father warns me against being so rash and demands to read it. I allow him to. And he is duly impressed. I am just so ready to get to a new level in my life as I sign it, scan it and send it back by email. I really need this, to change the dynamic of my life.

I celebrate my success with Scott. We get mildly tipsy on a couple of beers and chow down on some take-out pizza. Yet our celebration does not culminate in making love or even making out for that matter. For the most part he is cool with it. He understands I am taking a little break. The truth is I'm not sure I can make love again to Scott until I figure out what I am going to do about Hank. It's the only sexually ethical thing for me to do.

It has been cloudy and rainy for days and I have to walk Sweetie in the nighttime drizzle. Winter is approaching. When I get back in my bedroom and under the covers, I curl up on my side of the bed.

Scott gets up out of bed. He looks pissed off.

"Sylvia. I want to know what is going on. It has been weeks since we did it. And I want us to get busy again, you know?"

I am seeing his macho side manifest again and I am not sure how to respond.

"I am going through some private shit."

"But we are a team, baby. There shouldn't be anything private between us."

"I beg to differ on that one. I think, from my experience that no matter how close a couple is there must always be some boundaries. You must be patient with me. Now, come back to bed."

"No, I'm sorry, I cant. Not when I have this beastly hunger for your body. I need for you to soothe my savage soul."

"I'm not buying all this hungry he-man rhetoric. You just want to get laid. If you cannot stand being around me without us doing it then maybe we should take a little break."

"I don't want to take a break from you. You know how I feel about you. Look, let's get hitched."

"Oh, here we go again. You know I am not ready to get married again."

"You need somebody steady like me in your life after all that has happened to you."

"Only I know what I need. And I don't respond well to pressure. Now I'm going to sleep. Do what you want."

"Do you want me to split? Is that what you're getting at?"

"I didn't say that, you did."

"Okay, I can take a hint."

Scott puts on his clothes in a huff and just like that he is gone.

***

As the damp days pass, the leaves begin to fall.

One morning I look out my front window and I see

that same damn Porsche parked in front of my house again.

I make a sign that says, *Please don't park your car in front of my house, thank you,* and place it under the windshield wipers of the car.

I go shopping in TJ Max for a new winter coat. I treat myself to a cheap Sushi lunch at the Woodland Mall food court.

When I get home I put on the coat I bought and look at myself in the full-sized mirror.

I'm interrupted by the doorbell ringing. It is approaching evening and getting dark out. Without a second thought I take off the coat, go downstairs and open the front door. Standing in front of me is a man I don't recognize.

For a moment he takes my breath away. He is strikingly handsome in a way that I have never encountered before. He has a square jaw and eyes so blue they make me gasp. He is tall as well. Well over six feet. He is dressed in grey slacks and a freshly ironed, crisp, white shirt and a suede jacket.

"You don't know me," he says with a smirk. Like he is cocksure any woman will instantly get wet for him.

"No shit Sherlock," I joke back.

"I just want to respond to the message you sent me. If you are the one that sent me the message."

"Sent you a message? I have no idea what you are talking about."

"Did you write this?" It is only now that I notice he holds a sheet of paper in one hand. He shows me the very note I had written.

"You asked me to move my car. And I came to apologize to you for parking in front of your house."

Now that I see the actual owner of that mysterious and slightly annoying black Porsche is hot as hell I find I am much more understanding.

"Well, it's not that big a deal," I say. "It's just that in the winter it blocks the plows. And that's also where my friends park when they visit me. I like to keep it clear."

"Totally fine by me."

I further dig myself into a hole when I say, "From what I know of the law a car is not allowed to be parked any longer than forty-eight hours in one spot on the street. Just in case you thought I was being unreasonable."

"On the contrary, Miss, I am one-hundred percent hearing you. I can explain why I keep parking there. You see I have been house hunting in the area and I have had my eyes on a rental. And it may sound strange but before I move in anywhere I need to get a feel for the area. The only way I can do that is to walk around and observe. It's a big deal moving to a new neighborhood. And I have had some bad experiences. So if you must know I have been walking around, knocking on doors, seeing what folks think of the place."

"So you have been casing my neighborhood?" I ask, teasingly. "What are your conclusions?"

"There are some real good people here. Some have even invited me into their home and made me coffee. Others have been more reticent but for the most part I get very good vibes about this street."

"So are you going to rent the house?"

"I already did. I rented that house right across the street from yours."

He points to the understated two-story house. A family had been living there. I had no idea it had been put up for rent.

"I never even saw a realtors sign on that house." I say.

"I found the listing online. The owner's moved out

a while ago."

"Well, congrats."

"Thanks. I officially move in tomorrow. As you know there is no parking on that side of the street so that's why I have been parking in front of your house. Now that I'm the official tenant I can park in my own driveway. Listen, to make it up to you I would like to invite you to my new place for a little house warming tomorrow night. How does that sound?"

"Sounds lovely," I say. "What would you like me to bring?"

"Just yourself. I'm having a couple of people over. Not a big crowd. I would be honored if you came."

"My name is Sylvia. And yours?"

"I'm Phil. It is a pleasure to meet you Sylvia, and I look forward to seeing you tomorrow."

I nod goodbye and watch as he gets in his car and drives off.

***

I decide to dress simply all in black on the evening of the housewarming. I put on an oversized black sweater over leggings with knee-high boots. I apply my makeup, giving myself a smokey-eyed look, along with orange lipstick. When I am all ready I cross the street and knock on the door, noting the Porsche on his driveway.

Phil opens the door dressed in a football Jersey and a pair of jeans. He seems genuinely happy to see me.

"Sylvia, come in."

"Now I know where to get some sugar if I run out."

"People never run out of sugar. I don't know why they claim neighbors give each other sugar. Must have been from the old days or something."

His house, from what I can see is mostly barren.

He notices my curiosity and says, "Excuse my empty home. When I moved out of my other house I sold all my junky old furniture. I decided to start fresh and go modern. My IKEA shipment should come in a few weeks."

The dining room contains a foldable table and a few plastic lawn chairs. I can smell something cooking. Whatever it is, it smells delicious.

"I'm not much of a cook. But I put on a batch of pasta," he says.

What I want to ask is, "Where is everybody?"

"Would you like some wine?" Phil asks.

"Sure."

"Red or white?"

"Red will be fine."

He steps into the kitchen and comes back with a paper cup filed with slightly vinegary smelling cabernet sauvignon. Clearly not top of the line.

Then I think I hear a knock at the door. The sound puts me more at ease. Phil goes to the door and opens it. I hear him say something. I hear another voice. And then he closes the door again.

In his hand he holds an Amazon package.

"I ordered myself a Chanel Sweater."

He opens the package to reveal the colorful piece of clothing.

"What do you think?"

"Nice."

"I may as well put it on now. You might want to look away," he jokes.

I pretend to cover my eyes with my hands, while peeking through my fingers. He takes off his Jersey and I get a quick view of his torso. He is ripped. Clearly this guy works out. He slips on the sweater, tells me I can look now and I lower my hands.

We don't say anything for a moment. I feel a bit awkward.

He tells me he's a defense lawyer with a passion for the underdog and that many times he will take on cases pro bono if he can "stick it to the man" as he puts it. I am impressed by Phil's line of work but mostly I am growing increasingly uncomfortable with the fact that I am alone with a stranger. I am beginning to suspect this has all been a ploy to get me on my own when there is another knock on the door.

It's Shanice, the middle-aged black woman who lives next door to me. We often chat when we work on our lawns. She is the single mother of a college-aged girl.

Shanice steps in Phil's house holding a small package. When she sees me she says, "Oh, hello Sylvia. Fancy seeing you here." She pauses and I wonder if she senses the discomfort between me and Phil but then she adds, "I just came here to drop off some chocolates as my welcome to the neighborhood gift. I really can't stay."

"Are you sure, Shanice?" I say.

"Yeah, gotta run. Cooking dinner for my girl," she says.

At this point I really want to leave with her.

"I think I might get going. I will walk you out," I say to her.

"Hold on a sec?" Phil says. "Don't you want some lasagna?" he asks, so loudly and clearly to me that I figure it would be rude to say no.

My mouth waters and my stomach grumbles. Maybe I am on edge because I am hungry. So Shanice leaves and I stay.

Phil serves us both in plastic bowls and I eat with a plastic fork. More time passes and just as I suspected it has become clear that nobody else is coming.

Did he even invite anyone else?

I notice marinara sauce on Phil's chin.

"You have a bit of something on your chin," I say.

"Oh, thanks," he says, wiping it off with his hand.

"I'm sorry, nobody has showed. You must think I don't have any friends. Which isn't true. It's just that this whole thing was last minute. I only thought of this yesterday. You were the first person I invited. You know how busy people are. You have to give them warning. I might have to try this again with proper planning. But I'm glad you came."

It feels more like a date. I have downed three glasses of cheap red wine and we have both indulged in Shanice's delectable truffles and I am starting to adapt to the stark setting of unopened boxes and plastic furniture.

I notice that his empty house isn't as drafty as I would expect. In fact I feel warm all over, my cheeks slightly flushed.

"Are you sorry you came over?"

"Not at all. It has been great to meet you. Truthfully I don't know my neighbors as well as I should."

We share an awkward silence and it dawns on me that maybe I have overstayed my welcome.

"Well, I guess I am getting a bit tired," Phil says abruptly. "So I think I'm gong to call it a night."

I am surprised he is the one cutting this short. He is right though. It's about time I got on home. It's the only proper thing to do.

He walks me to the door where he says, "I have a confession to make," as he reaches for the doorknob.

"What is that?" I ask, tipsily. It's a good thing I don't have to drive home. All I have to do is make it across the street.

"The only other person that I invited was Shanice. She is a cool lady. I sensed she wouldn't stay very long. We have worked together on some cases. She is a legal activist as well. It is a very small world."

The doorbell chimes, startling us both.

He opens the door. Outside, dry leaves are whirling around in the wind.

A few cars go by. Headlight beams blinding light into my eyes.

Phil's guest steps out of the headlight's glare and into the house and my lungs freeze.

CHAPTER THIRTY

DR MEADOWS

Phil introduces us.

"Sylvia, this is Dr. Bert Meadows."

She looks nervous. She shuffles on her feet and mutters, "Yes, we have already met.

I sense she feels uncomfortable. Which is totally understandable under the circumstances.

"She is correct. Sylvia and I have already met. But I am not at liberty to say where. But Sylvia, I would like you to know that sometimes I have to see things with my own eyes. I cannot rely only on what a patient claims about their condition."

"Oh, I get it," Phil says. "Don't tell me, she is a patient of yours?"

"A former patient," she says.

"How do the two of you know each other?" she asks. She leans against a wall as if to steady herself.

"From the Y," Phil says. "We both lift."

"Correction, Phil lifts," I interrupt. "I mostly just dabble around taking in the ambiance of the gym. I am certainly not the strong-man that he is," I say.

"You sell yourself short, Bert. You may not be very muscular but you are in great cardiovascular shape for a man your age."

"*For a man my age* it is an accomplishment just to be above ground."

"Please, you talk like you're an old man. You have some good years ahead of you," Phil says.

"Thanks, but I am smart enough to know that my best years are behind me."

Sylvia loses her balance then rights herself.

"Listen," she says, while reaching for the front doorknob. "I really have to get home. I have to feed my dog. She has a little stomach upset and her feeding schedule is all screwed up. Phil, welcome to the block. I'm sure you're going to love it here."

"Are you sure you have to go so soon," I say, noticing she has omitted saying goodbye to me.

I thought this would be the perfect time to perform my intervention. Yet from the facial signals that Phil is sending my way, I sense that he thinks the timing isn't right. I am not an impatient man. I understand that it will take some time to snatch her with my butterfly net.

"Okay, well, it was great to see you Sylvia."

She walks out the door. And we both watch as she crosses the lamp-lit street, checking her mail before she puts the key in her door.

CHAPTER THIRTY-ONE

SYLVIA

There is only one envelope in my mailbox. I examine it. There is no postage stamp on it so I presume whoever sent it hand delivered it. It must be junk mail. I enter my house. Sweetie greets me. I pick her up and allow her to cover my face with licks.

I close my front curtains and flop down on my couch. Sweetie jumps up and snuggles beside me. I open the envelope and begin to read the letter that is inside:

Dear Sylvia,

Please forgive my intrusion into your personal life by hand delivering this letter to your home. I usually don't pursue those who I hope to help.

And help is exactly what you need. Sometimes we psychiatrists must research our clients. In your case this has required some footwork and my putting on the private detective hat. I won't tell you how I know. But I know that you are acting out right now in your life. You have told me about Scott, a genuinely good man who loves you. You have not told me, but I am aware of Hank, the millionaire that so easily swept you off your feet in Manhattan and with whom you have signed a two year deal. What you are doing is engaging in risky sexual behavior with no regard to the consequences which could result in you having an unwanted pregnancy or possibly contracting an STD. Don't think you are immune. We are all susceptible.

The problem isn't necessarily what you are doing now. But as your condition worsens things could become increasingly precarious. You might suffer auditory or visual hallucinations or moments of such grandiosely that you might actually do something that gets you into trouble with the law. Or something which might bring about your own bodily harm or once again, harm another. I don't want this to happen to you.

*Sincerely yours,
Dr. Bert Meadows.*

I throw the letter on the floor and feel for a moment like I cannot catch my breath.

Suddenly, for the first time, I feel unsafe. Alone. Like I had better get somebody on my side soon. Somebody who I *know* can protect me. My first inclination is to call Hank and ask him to take the next flight out. How will Scott feel about this? What about Scott? I should call and ask him to come over.

I text him instead.

Please come over as soon as you can. I want to see you.

I wait for an answer then text him again.

I need you.

Is he still angry with me for turning him down in bed? Or because of my unwillingness to commit to marriage?

I call him but he doesn't pick up.

I should call 911 and report the letter from Dr. Meadows. I weigh that option. He is a registered psychiatrist. If they read his letter they might side with him. They could perceive me as being the one out of balance.

I turn out all the lights and peek through the curtains. I can barely make out what is happening at the house across the street. From what I can see Phil is still standing in his own front window chatting with Dr. Meadows. I mean what are the chances of the two of them knowing each other? It occurs to me that maybe the two of them are in cahoots.

It isn't long before I decide to text Hank. I'm going to need as much help as I can get.

I need your advice.

I am surprised when he responds right away.

What's up?

Can we talk?

I am in the middle of a meeting. Can you tell me what this is about?

It is hard to explain in a text. It's my former therapist. He's been leaving me voicemails. I just ran into him at a neighbor's. Then I found a hand-delivered letter from him in my mailbox.

Try to stay calm. If you feel in immediate danger

call the police. Otherwise I'll give you a ring in two hours.

A few minutes later Dr. Meadows is leaving Phil's house. Does Phil know what he's up to? Maybe I should cross the street and bring it all out in the open. But might I come off as unhinged? After all, Phil doesn't really know me. And he *is* Dr. Meadows' friend. What if he sides with him? Even worse, what if Dr. Meadows has told Phil about me? Or exaggerated or even lied to him?

Dr. Meadows crosses the street towards my house. Does he really have the balls to come over here and ring my doorbell right in front of Phil?

It seems not. He goes to his car which is parked in front of Shanice's house next door and gets in. He doesn't even look my way. He idles the car a while then drives off.

Phil stands in the light of his doorway. He looks right and left, then closes his door, his entry light switching off.

CHAPTER THIRTY-TWO

WILL

The way my wife is carrying on I feel as though she is trying to make me turn over in my grave. She hurriedly crosses the street in front of oncoming traffic and narrowly misses early death which would bring her to me sooner. A car screeches to a halt and the front lights almost tap her on her hips. She is illuminated which makes her look like the madwoman that Dr. Meadows is telling her she is. Now, I am not so sure that I can keep watching. I'm afraid she won't make it. It's not easy being me, to be stuck in utter isolation, tormented by what you see but can do nothing about.

Rather than ring the doorbell she instead pounds on the door until Phil answers.

"Listen, Phil. I need to talk to you about Dr. Meadows."

"You mean Bert?"

"Yes, Bert. Is that guy on the level? You said you met him at the gym? Are you really good friends?"

"What is this all about, Sylvia? You seem upset."

"Please answer my question."

"Okay. Well, I would say we are gym buddies. We have gone out for drinks a few times but that's about it."

"He knows where you live?"

"Yes."

"He is harassing me."

"Oh?"

"I came over here, he turns up, I go home, check my mailbox and he's written and hand-delivered a letter to me!"

"Right."

"I just want to know if you know what is up with this creepy psychiatrist. I need answers," she says.

He asks her to wait, leaves her standing on the doorstep. He returns seconds later holding a pistol with a silencer on it.

She opens her mouth to scream but he presses the barrel against her stomach, drags her inside his house and shuts the door.

"Upstairs," he says.

She has no choice but to do as she's told.

Once he's got her in the bedroom he goes over to the window to pull down the blind, keeping the pistol aimed at her.

He retrieves a rope from the closet.

"What's that for?" she asks, swallowing noisily.

He moves swiftly, grabbing a wrist and proceeding to bind it.

"Hey! What are you doing?"

Within seconds he has fastened her wrist to the other, and with a knot, has tied both to her ankles. He works so expertly that he is positive he has done this before.

She tries to wriggle free, too dumbfounded to speak.

CHAPTER THIRTY-THREE

SCOTT

I sense something in Sylvia's text that tells me I should – rather than texting back – simply show up at her house. I know I am speeding as I drive there and that's because I feel something is wrong. I figure it might be something to do with her dog. She loves Sweetie. If the dog so much as throws up then it is off to the vet she goes. Lately Sweetie has been spacing out a bit now and again – staring at walls and into corners. I tell her it's just the way senior dogs act. Dogs get senile just like people do. Anyhow it just turned out her dog wasn't feeling well. Sweetie's cognitive abilities are back to normal. Thank God. Because when something is wrong with her dog something is very much wrong with my Sylvia. In some ways that dog is like our child. I feel like I am Sweetie's stepfather.

When I arrive at Sylvia's house, I am relieved to see her car parked in her driveway. I hop out of my car, walk to her front door and ring the bell. I wait a while before using the spare key she gave me so that I could house and dog sit while she was in New York. I figure she might be in the shower or napping. I'm hoping that whatever emergency there might have been has now passed.

Was it the plumbing in the kitchen sink again? Her disposal is always on the blink. When it goes askew it gargles like a trapped beast. I've had to plunge it for her a few times.

Sweetie saunters in from the living room and greets me with enthusiasm. Her dog knows my scent.

I stoop down and pet her. She licks my hand, her tail wagging.

I check the living room, dining room and kitchen. Sylvia is nowhere to be found. I take the stairway two steps at a time and check her bedroom and the door to the bathroom is open. Hmm, maybe she is downstairs doing laundry?

I go down the two flights to the laundry room. She's not here either.

Her car is here yet she is nowhere to be found.

I head back to the first floor and step out into the backyard, I even check her garage art studio where she paints still lives and landscapes. She's not there either.

So I go back inside and start to brood as to where she could be. My mind races through all the variables. Is she visiting a next door neighbor? That is unlikely as she keeps her relations with her neighbors at a friendly, cordial minimum. I am positively stumped and figure my best course of action is to make myself some coffee and wait for her to turn up, which I've no doubt she will.

I make and finish my coffee and maybe a half hour or so passes and as she hasn't shown up and with the caffeine working up my anxiety, I deduce like a half-baked Sherlock that maybe she accidentally cut herself in the kitchen while opening some canned food, called 911 for an ambulance and she's at the ER right now getting stitches and a tetanus shot. I wouldn't put it past her as she is accident prone as well as squeamish around blood. She is a bit of a hypochondriac who often fears she will get Salmonella from the cutting board where she has chopped some raw chicken. She will wash it and powder it with Ajax. I don't know if she's always been like this or if it results from the event that led to her widowhood, but Sylvia is slightly preoccupied with her own mortality.

I deduce waiting for her to provide me with an explanation as to her whereabouts is my best option, so I lie down on her couch.

I awake at 10 p.m. to discover that sometime during my snooze Sweetie crawled up to join me. She remains snoring at my feet.

Sylvia is still not home.

I leave the couch and check to see if she has retrieved today's mail. During the days she was gone I collected it for her each morning.

I lean out the front door and check the box. I notice there is one envelope among a pile of junk that is unmarked, which means it must have been hand-delivered. In fact it is not even sealed. Now, I am not the sort to open other people's post, not even that of my own girlfriend but these are extenuating circumstances.

I throw caution to the wind and open it up. Inside is a letter. I turn on the light and sit at her dining room table to read it.

Dear Sylvia,

I am not giving up on you. So many times I see those who come to me for help but I see something special in you. People such as yourself who are what we term "noncompliant." And I confess, I have taken a personal interest in you. Some may see you as having a mental illness but I see you as a very unique woman. It is as simple as that. And I want to protect you from having a decline in your ability to reason with reality, which might result in catastrophic harm, either to yourself or to others. In your case, I alone can save you.

Once a person like yourself has crossed the line and have killed they no longer have the same boundaries that an average person has. Especially when the legal system has given them a "free pass" so to speak. I find the fact that you have killed a man utterly fascinating. And it makes me want to spend more alone time with you. Together we can achieve a kind of nirvana. We can both share in your unique psychological disposition.

And so I ask once more that you schedule a visit with me in my office at your earliest convenience.

Call or text me as soon as you can, please.

Best wishes,
Dr. Meadows.

I bury my face in my hands. This letter comes as a total shock to me. Though Sylvia can be erratic at times, I never suspected she suffered from mental illness. For a psychiatrist to reach out to her in this strangely personal manner must mean something very serious is going on with her that she has not told me about. Also I can see from this letter that there is something definitely wrong with this psychiatrist. And yet when she comes home I cannot tell her that I read this letter, which I place back in its envelope and deposit back into the mailbox. I don't want her to think I am all up in her personal affairs. All I can do now is try to steer a conversation towards the subject of her psychological wellbeing and hope that she divulges this to me. But I am alarmed by this letter. And I must, if I can, discourage her from continuing her therapy with this man who is clearly deluded.

As midnight approaches, I am about as worried as I can get. I have texted her pretty much every half an hour like a neurotic boyfriend. Which I am not. I consider myself to be a strong person, physically and mentally. Confident, assertive, a good problem-solver. But right now I am at a loss as to what to do. Should I go out and search for her? Involve the police?

What if she's having a nervous breakdown? What if alerting the authorities is the wrong thing to do? I just don't know. And it's that – not knowing – that paralyses me.

CHAPTER THIRTY-FOUR

HANK

I asked Angelique to get in touch with the pilots of my private jet. She arranges for them to fly me out of LaGuardia at five o'clock tomorrow morning, which is fine by me since I rarely sleep more than four hours a night as it is. I'm a light sleeper. Easily woken. And I don't need much of it. Most days I wake before sunrise and have gotten the lion's share of my work done before noon. I know for a fact that sacrificing sleep for work has led to my media empire. And still, even with all that I have: a luxury apartment in New York, a beachfront property in Bermuda and a little getaway cottage on Lake Michigan, I still feel I can do better, have more, and that if I even so much as slack off just a little bit I will lose it all in a heartbeat.

I pack light and am at the airport by 4 a.m. During the flight I keep myself busy on my laptop working on some more deals that will benefit Sylvia. She is my latest project and so there is much to be done.

I question whether I should have slept with her. But it just happened. And sometimes things happen. I have never subscribed to the whole casting couch thing. Yet, I have slept with a few of my employees. I pray it will not come back to bite me. So far I have had nothing but amicable breakups – some of which cost me a little just to make sure the woman felt valued as she took her leave from my life. It's amazing the sort of goodwill that can be created by purchasing a gal a Ford Mustang GT.

I have texted Sylvia a few more times and she has not responded to a single text since her alarming first one. Due to the late notice there is no flight attendant for this last-minute trip. So I fix myself a Diet Coke over ice and get back in my seat.

Now I am a bit worried. When I take on a new client, or a new lover I don't treat it as a casual thing. I mean business in every department. At this point in my life and career, every relationship has value to me. I am more than just a "people person." People are the life blood of my agency. And I also appreciate the value of every human being that steps in front of me. Why? Well, because many people are responsible for getting me where I am. I have rarely burned any bridges.

Once in Grand Rapids, I exit the plane to a dreary, cloudy, day with a cold drizzle. An Uber is waiting for me. I rather like this town. And would consider buying property here just as an investment since it has a reputation as having a hot market for new homeowners.

I arrive at her home, climb from the car and stand in front of her house. I step up to the front door, ring the buzzer and wait.

The door opens to a rustic-looking guy with thick, brown hair and wrinkled slept-in clothing. He looks like he has gotten out of bed.

With Sylvia?

He opens the screen door and I get a better look at him. He has stubble on his square jaw, and I acknowledge that this guy is the sort women swoon

for.
"Hello, my name is Hank. I represent Sylvia."
"I'm Scott, her boyfriend."

CHAPTER THIRTY-FIVE

SYLVIA

My hands and feet are bound and I have gauze-like cloth gagging me. Phil just locked the door last night leaving me here, in this state. I managed to chew a hole in the gauze, so that I could at least breathe comfortably. I slept fitfully, exhausted from my predicament. A few splashes of light filter in through the closed curtain. I have no idea what time it is.

The door opens. Phil enters the room with a glass of water in one hand and his gun in his other. He undoes the rag across my mouth as he presses the barrel of his gun against my forehead.

"I can't offer you coffee just yet, but I don't want you to get thirsty." He props me up against the wall and puts the glass of water to my lips. "You don't want to get dehydrated. You have enough problems as it is."

I worry that he might have drugged it.

"I said drink."

I feel the gun barrel hard against my forehead.

I do as he says. The water is lukewarm but I can't detect a flavor to it. It just tastes like tap water to me.

Phil is now pacing back and forth in the bedroom.

"What are you doing Phil? Just let me go. I won't

tell anyone what you've done, which so far is only tie me up. You go your way and I go mine."

"You mean just allow you to live across the street so that you can do as you please?"

"I will happily move away if that is what you want. I have the means to do that."

"So I have heard. We know all about you. About the three mil you got as a settlement for murdering your husband."

"If it is money you want, I will gladly give you some."

"That's not what I am after."

"What do *you* want? Tell me."

He covers my mouth again and I try to speak but my voice is muffled.

"Breakfast will be served in a bit. I am not here to starve you either."

He leaves the room once more, returning some time later with a plastic plate containing sunny side up fried eggs, bacon and burnt toast and a Styrofoam cup of black coffee. He unwraps the gag from my mouth so that I can eat it.

"Breakfast is served," he says, with the same good-natured warmth to his voice that he used when we first meet. It's also the gentlemanly quality that seduced me into this predicament.

Tears fill my eyes and cascade down my cheeks.

He brings a forkful of food to my closed lips but I refuse it by turning my face away. The breakfast looks like prison food and I have zero appetite.

"Why are you doing this?" I say.

He sets the plate of food down on the floor and wipes the tears from my face. If I wasn't tied up I would push his hand away. I'll bite him if he tries to touch me again.

"People are going to look for me. How long do you

think you can get away with this?"

"I don't need long for what I want to do."

"And what is that?"

"Here, have some of this."

He picks up some greasy bacon and tries to force-feed me a forkful of it. I turn my face away. He's a lousy cook.

"No thanks."

"Suit yourself. It's not very polite of you though, considering all the trouble I went through to prepare this for you."

He reapplies the gag and leaves the room once more.

I lie there praying. I was brought up Catholic and I am getting mighty religious mighty fast.

I feel a presence watching over me again. I wonder who it could be. I wish my mother was still alive to protect me now. I wish I was a little girl and I could start everything all over again. This time I would heed my mommy's warnings about the boys being no good for my health.

I feel like she is here with me. I often feel her around. We had a very strong bond. They say there is nothing like the bond between a mother and her daughter.

CHAPTER THIRTY-SIX

ANNE

"I am right here with you my beautiful daughter," is what I wish I could tell Sylvia right now.

I have watched over her all night long and I am watching over her now. All I can pray for is that she is in no pain. It cannot be comfortable to be tied and gagged like that. That monster is currently downstairs just casually making himself some instant coffee and eating a stale cookie. Phil opens his fridge to check if there is anything better to eat. Searching inside again he only sees the food that the previous renters left behind. Just some out-of-date milk, rotten cottage cheese and some rancid chicken salad that has become nothing more than poison. It's a good thing Sylvia refused the food he prepared. She would become sick for sure.

Phil sits on a plastic chair with his coffee. It looks like he is thinking, planning. I have no idea what he is going to do to my daughter. If he kills her she will come here. Yet I don't know if that means I will get to see her again. I have no clue how this after death thing works. And I don't wish this upon her. I want her to go on to have a happy life. I am in no hurry to see her here, with me. I wonder if I am her guardian.

Am I supposed to welcome her at the gates to eternity? Is it my job to make sure she has a safe passage? I don't want any of that. I want only life, love, and health for her.

Holding his instant coffee he walks upstairs again. He enters her room and finds her futilely trying to undo the knots that bind her.

"Listen to me Sylvia," Phil says, after a sip of coffee, "I don't want you to hate me. Really, I'm not such a bad person. I'm just have a job to do. I am nothing but a hired hand. I'm just trying to make a living. So I do jobs. You know, ugly, dirty jobs. But like garbage men, or janitors, somebody has got to do it. Somebody has to get their hands dirty for the rest of us to live cleanly. People get in touch with me, you know, when they have something nasty that needs to get done. And that's what I do."

My daughter's eyes are wide and bloodshot. She can barely breathe. She so much wants to speak. To attempt to reason with him. She struggles so much that Phil says, "I see there is something you want to tell me, and I very much like to hear what it is."

He removes her gag and she gasps for air and then manages to eek out the words, "I have far more money than whatever it is you are being paid. I can make you a very rich man if you let me go."

"You want to negotiate."

He peeks out through the blinds to where two cars are parked in front of Sylvia's house. One of the cars is parked in the driveway. This tips him off that people know she's missing. From the expression on his face, he must know he doesn't have much time to either carry through with his plan or make a sudden change of course.

"What you are suggesting is temping. There is nothing holding me to this town. And yeah, I could grab my passport and disappear. Though I'd hate to leave my two Pitbull's behind."

I know when he mentions his dogs that Sylvia must be thinking about Sweetie. I wish I could tell her that Scott fed her before he fell asleep. But all I can do is watch and listen, helplessly, which isn't easy for a mother to do. My job has always been to protect her. A year ago, when I couldn't, she took care of the situation herself.

"I think I like your idea. The problem is my partner has already been dispatched. And once he gets here there is no turning back. So, we would have to get out of here now if I take you up on your offer."

"Then untie me."

He sets his coffee mug down in the corner of the room, gets on his knees and begins to untie her.

Downstairs, somebody begins pounding at the door.

CHAPTER THIRTY-SEVEN

SCOTT

I have actually invited this Hank guy into Sylvia's house. He is dressed in khaki pants, a grey T-shirt and a form-fitting black blazer. His wears designer tennis shoes that are probably signed by a sports superstar. He has the vibe of a guy with bucks. I can spot them every time. He is calm and collected and starts controlling the conversation right away.

"Listen, I came out here on short notice. She texted me," Hank says.

"So you fly out all the way from New York City just because Sylvia texted you? You two must be tight," I say.

"You could say that. We believe in her."

"We? As in who?"

"As in my company. We represent relevant personalities as well as products."

"Sylvia is not just a personality or a product. She's a real person. And I think something is wrong. She never came home last night."

Hank looks me up and down. He is as curious about me as I am of him. Suspicious too.

"So how long have you two been together?" he dares to ask me.

"None of your fucking business. Are you a detective? Am I the suspect? Shit, man. She also sent me a text and I have been waiting for her all night."

"Okay, has she ever done this before?"

"No, she hasn't done this before. If you must know she's a real homebody. So this just isn't like her."

"Have you called the cops?"

"Nope, not yet. I was waiting for her to get home, hopeful there was a good explanation. Should I call them?"

"Maybe. Have you tried to call her this morning?"

"As a matter of fact I haven't," I say. "I figured that since she has not answered any of my texts then she won't answer a call. I mean why blow up her phone? Maybe she is, I don't know, off with some other guy?"

"So you don't have an exclusive relationship?" Hanks asks me.

"Of course we do."

Hank looks around the entryway of Sylvia's house. As if he might find clues somewhere. Then he walks into the living room and stares out the bay window at the house across the street. "We have to do something about this," Hank says. "Does she have family in the area?"

"Only her father."

"What about her mother?"

"Her mom died a few years back."

"I see."

"Do you have her father's number?"

"As a matter of fact, I do. I think it's on my phone. Let me check. Hold on a sec."

And then I leave this Hank guy who I suspect is sleeping with my woman where he stands to head up the stairs to fetch my phone from the nightstand. I scroll through my contacts until I find his number, then hit the staircase.

"I will call him now."

Sylvia's father doesn't pick up. Who does anymore? You could be ready to jump off a bridge and be making your last call for help and nobody would answer their damn phone.

I text her dad.

Mr. Henderson, this is Scott. Is Sylvia over there with you? Please return this call as soon as you can.

I return downstairs where Hank is still gazing through the window.

"I take it he didn't pick up," Hank says.

"Nope."

I walk towards Hank and look out the window as well. I see a guy dressed all in black standing in front of the door of the house across the street. From what I can see he is dressed in leather pants and a leather jacket with the logo of an Eagle on the breast. He looks like a biker. Like he a member of the *Hell's Angels.* Then I notice the souped-up Harley parked on the driveway. From what I know, the house across the street is still occupied by a very quiet, private family. They have always seemed like suburban zombies to me. Totally oblivious to anybody else. Come to think of it I have not seen them there in a while. Never thought about it before. Who knows, maybe they moved. Maybe we missed the moment when the u-hauls came for their shit. The guy in leather is a big guy. He must weigh about two-sixty. He has a bald head and a thick neck. Some guy I have never seen before lets him in the house.

"Do you know those folks across the street?" Hank asks.

"A family has lived there for a couple of years. They keep to themselves."

"Have you ever seen that thug before?"

"Naw, never. Maybe he's their crazy uncle."

We both laugh for a moment, nervously.

"Should we take a wait and see approach?" I suggest.

"We could but I am a bit more proactive than that."

"Wanna call the cops?"

"My gut tells me not to. I have a feeling that Sylvia is just going through something emotionally."

"So now you are up on Sylvia's emotions? Did the two of you share a few emotions while she was out there in New York City?"

"I won't even dignify your questions and their implications with an answer."

"Why the fuck not? I mean, from what I can tell, you have some funds in your account. I can spot guys like you every time. The sort that plays down what they've got. Maybe you're afraid of being a target or of people taking advantage of you. I'm sure you wined and dined my girlfriend. Impressed her real good. I bet I didn't measure up against you, after a few drinks. Even though I own my company I must seem like a real nobody compared to you, a bigwig, living I'm sure, in the lap of luxury. Did you fuck her?"

"Listen, I didn't sign up for the nth degree. I am here for Sylvia. This is not going to do us any good."

"You can leave if you like."

"If she is in trouble I can help."

"How?"

"I don't know."

I remember the letter. And suddenly it's not so important that I accuse this guy of stealing my woman. I should tell Hank about it. Maybe he can make heads or tails out of its implications. I drop the jealous boyfriend routine and say, "Okay, listen. There is something I think you should see." I retrieve the letter from the mailbox and hand it to him.

"Do you mind if I sit down while I read this?" he says.

"Be my guest."

"Thank you."

He sits down and reads it quickly.

"I think we have a problem here. This could be serious. If this doctor is so concerned with Sylvia's mental state that he would drop a letter off here at her place of residence then this really is concerning. Maybe she has harmed herself or is about to."

"I can see how you might think that," I say. "But I know Sylvia a little better than you do. And I can assure you she is a stable woman. More stable than a lot of women I have dated. And considering what she has been through, I would say she is pretty damn adjusted."

"Yes, but you are her boyfriend and not her doctor."

"Did you notice anything off about her when she was in New York?"

"I really don't know. I mean we had a good time. She seemed happy."

"I really don't need to hear this. Did she fucking cheat on me?"

"Please relax, I assure you my interest in her is strictly professional. But that doesn't mean I don't care about her."

I know this rich dude is lying through his teeth. Chances are they spent the whole weekend in bed together, ordering room service. The son of a bitch! I could take a swing at him right this second. Give him a good blow to the jaw that might knock out a few teeth. Yet, I am sure it isn't all his fault. Sylvia surely shares some of the blame. Chances are she gave him some cues. All women do. Men don't just bust moves without the woman giving a few salacious hints. Well, not all men. Some men just go in for the kill. But this guy has a reputation to think of.

Hank keeps staring out the window at that house across the street.

The Harley is still there. The rotund biker type has apparently gone inside the house.

"I suggest we just stay put right here," Hank says. "She will come home eventually. I trust she will not do anything rash."

"It's not like her to leave her dog unattended. That's really why I'm worried. Sometimes I think she loves Sweetie more than me," I say.

Hank's jaw clenches.

CHAPTER THIRTY-EIGHT

SYLVIA

Gagged and bound as I am, I can still just barely hear Phil answer his door downstairs. He is engaging in a conversation with a man who has a very low, husky voice. He returns upstairs and I am untied and allowed to stand upright on my bare feet. All I can do is wonder in fright as to what this freak has in store for me next.

Phil tosses the rope across the mattress he didn't even bother to cover with a sheet that I was forced to sleep on last night. "You're a very lucky girl. Because most of my projects never know what hit 'em. I just take care of what I have to do. It isn't my job to give you an explanation. Just one minute you are here. And the next you're in that . . . well, that great beyond."

I don't know how to reply. I'm too afraid of saying the wrong thing. After all he's holding a gun in his hand. One wrong word, one wrong move, and I will find out exactly what comes after all of this. I am afraid of dying. Very afraid. I love my life. My dog Sweetie. My modest house. I miss my mother but I still have my dad. I have money in the bank. Enough to last a long time. And then there's Hank. He has given me a renewed purpose, a useful way to spend my days. And as for Scott, it touches me deeply that he loves me so much. He too might just be what I need. I don't want to die. I'm not finished living.

There is a soft knock at the door that sends shivers through my body.

"Come in, it's not locked."

The door creaks open and in walks a huge leather-clad guy who reminds me of the bikers I often see at local dives. The ones who cuss at the sports channels on the big screen TVs. The kind of guys who might go so far as to dare to grab my ass as I walk past them. He has a hairy neck that is heavily tattooed. In fact he is as hairy as a Chia Pet.

"Hey, girl," he says to me. His voice has the rasp of a heavy smoker. He reeks of tobacco and liquor.

I scowl at him.

CHAPTER THIRTY-NINE

DR MEADOWS

With my extensive experience in pathology I am well aware of the difference between neurosis and psychosis. Neurotics are looking for answers and a way to escape the madness and depression that consumes them. Psychotics move into their illness, embrace it and think the rest of the world are mad. I know associates of mine who, I am afraid, would diagnose me as the latter. I am moving in for the object of my fixation. And that object is Sylvia. It has been this way since I first set eyes on her.

It is never a good thing when a patient is not an advocate for her own mental health. And since she has not contacted me back I have taken matters into my own hands. Once again my methods are not orthodox but then again no intervention is. I am driving over to her house to see her. I cannot let her slip between the cracks. The fact that I have fallen deeply in love with everything about her is not the point. The satisfaction I get from the work I do is derived from knowing that I have made a difference to someone's life. And by doing so it makes me feel validated as a human being. The paradox is not lost on me.

I notice there is a car parked in Sylvia's driveway. But it doesn't concern me. I am returning to Phil's home across the street. I have some personal business to take care of.

After I park my car, I walk to the front door and ring the doorbell.

I feel closer than ever to capturing and keeping Sylvia.

CHAPTER FORTY

SCOTT

I now suspect Hank of somehow being responsible for Sylvia's sudden disappearance. And I tell him so.

"What happened with you and Sylvia in New York? Something must have happened there to upset her. As we now know she is in a fragile state."

"Oh please, Scott. She had a wonderful time with me in the city. And by the way, I was the perfect gentleman."

"We all know the true intentions of 'perfect gentlemen' when they are around a beautiful woman like Sylvia."

"Let's not get all hot under the collar. This is not the time or the place for that."

"Something has pushed her over the edge."

"Look, once again you know her much better than I do. But Sylvia doesn't strike me as suicidal. She is a fucking survivor. In my opinion she is no victim."

"We have both read the letter from that psychiatrist. This guy sounds messed up to me. He is the one who needs to be on medication."

"Look," Hank says. "I don't know who this shrink is. But I have never trusted them. In my humble option the psychiatric community just wants to drug up everybody. They are in bed with the pharmaceutical companies. I am sure there are all sorts of kickbacks going on."

"Medication helped my sister," I tell Hank. "She was going through some bad shit when she was in college. Now she is happily married with kids. So they aren't all bad."

"Okay, Scott, so you know one good outcome. Your sister might have gotten better on her own. I know a few people that got all fucked up on those meds. One employee of mine got on that shit and became a zombie. He still works for me but he is so medicated now that he hardly even cracks a smile. He just stares into space most of the time. Sure he has a wife and kids too, but I don't think he gets anything out of the deal. Just about everything in that letter does not sit right with me. I have never heard of a reputable psychiatrist leaving a note in a person's mailbox."

As Hank speaks he seems transfixed by what he sees outside the window.

"I think we should call the cops," I suggest again.

"But what if she comes waltzing back here?" Hank says.

"Come on, if she needs help, she needs help," I insist.

"I won't allow it," Hank says. "From what I know of Sylvia, she is mentally and physically strong. Something else is going on here. You have to remember she is fairly well-known. Her story got around. It was all over the media for a while. Things might have died down, but there could still be some sicko somewhere that didn't like what he read about her."

"Why would someone take issue with what happened to her?" I ask Hank.

"I'm sure there are people out there who doubt

her story. I would see certain comments on threads when I came across her story online. There were people that thought she was making the whole thing up. That she was never abused by her husband at all. That it wasn't his gun. That it was her gun and she set him up. That it was all part of some evil plan."

"I never saw those comments. But then again I was not as aware of her fame when I met her. I don't do social media and avoid the news. I have always taken Sylvia at face value. Who cares what trolls have written? Those cowards never have the guts to identify themselves or show their faces."

"Maybe one of those trolls is not such a coward anymore. Maybe he has been stalking her. This world is a dangerous place for a strong woman like Sylvia," Hank says while still staring out the window.

Maybe he doesn't have the guts to look me in the eyes.

"Look, I hear what you are saying. You're talking about a whole lot of maybes. But man, I don't know you. I don't know what you're about. You fly out to her house with all these concerns for my girlfriend. Something doesn't sit right about you to me. What I am saying is that I know you have been with her."

"What makes you think that?"

This is the first time that Hank turns away from the bay window. The afternoon light hits him and I can see his appeal to women. He is a fit guy who radiates money. I can also tell he knows how to sweettalk a woman like Sylvia as well as sweeten the deal even more with the things that only cash can buy.

"No man can spend a whole weekend with an attractive woman and not want to sleep with her."

"You are her boyfriend. It is natural for you to think that way about Sylvia. Natural as well for you to be jealous. But I assure you I pose no threat to your relationship," Hank says. "Now, I suggest we knock on a couple of doors on the block. Maybe one of her neighbors might have seen her."

"Now you're playing detective. Isn't that the job for the police?"

"It's a hell of a lot better than getting cops involved. Look, I don't think there is anything wrong with her head. On the contrary. I think somebody might just be fucking with her head."

"Okay, let me get the dog's leash and bring her out with us. She's been cooped up all this time."

I leash Sweetie and we walk out the front door.

First we go next door and knock on Shanice's door. Sylvia chats with her all the time and even introduced us.

Shanice's college-age daughter answers the door.

"Hey," I say. I don't know her name. "Is your mom home?"

"Nah, she's out shopping."

"Have you seen Sylvia lately?"

"Not really, I just got back from school an hour ago. I can ask my mom when she gets back."

"Okay, thanks."

"Are you sure you haven't seen her?" Hank asks. I can see he is the pushy type of New Yorker.

"Is there something going on?" she asks.

"Don't know. Nobody has seen her for a while."

"Gee, I hope she's okay."

"Us too. Will you let us know if you hear from or see her?"

'No problem. I will ask my mom when she gets home if she knows anything."

"Thank you," Hanks says.

She closes the door. We walk over to the sidewalk.

Sweetie relieves herself on the grass. And then she

begins to bark even though there are no dogs or other people around. Sweetie rarely barks at all. She mainly only barks when she sees Sylvia. She is one of those rare dogs that bark with joy at the sight of her owner.

Right now the dog is barking at the house across the street. Wild, frantic barking.

"Is that dog okay?" Hank asks.

"She usually doesn't act this way. Really she only barks when she sees Sylvia. They're really close."

"Cute."

Sweetie keeps barking as we start to head towards the house on the other side of Sylvia's. She doesn't want to go this direction. She resumes barking. She is tugging at the leash so hard I almost lose my grip. She seems to be anxious to cross the street.

Hank observers this with great interest.

"Hey, why don't we see where her dog wants to go. Maybe she is picking up on her master's scent. In the meantime we can ask whoever lives across the street if they have seen Sylvia."

"Sure," I say. "Couldn't hurt."

CHAPTER FORTY-ONE

HANK

That dog of Sylvia's really wants to cross the street something bad. I have had my fair share of dogs. And one thing I can say is that they are much smarter than we think. In fact I think they can pick up on things on a deeper level than us mere humans. I have heard of dogs smelling cancer on their owners. We all know about the dogs that sniff out landmines and bombs. And how about the dogs they use to search for missing bodies? Well in this case we have an amateur canine sleuth on our hands. We don't need the cops to bring on the hounds. We have a mutt here that can do the trick.

Just as I suspect, the dog tugs at her leash until she has crossed the street and is standing in the yard of that innocuous two-story house. All the curtains and the blinds are down. When we get to the entry, Sylvia's dog starts pawing at the front door. That is when it dawns on me that we might be onto something.

From what little I know about her, I can say that Sylvia is a gregarious girl and my guess is that she is having a grand time with whoever lives here. I am sure she is friends with many who live in her neighborhood. Maybe she was hanging out and she drank too much while bragging about her deal with me, and fell asleep on their couch. I wouldn't put it past her. She is a free spirit. I myself didn't grow up until I turned forty. My twenties were a blur of crashing at friend's houses, getting way too drunk, smoking far too many cigarettes and puffing on far too many joints and yeah, snorting a line or two on a few downtown Tribeca after-club occasions.

I am the one who pushes the doorbell. We hear its muffled sound inside. We know for a fact that people are home here. We saw the hefty leather-clad dude go in. There are two cars parked in front, plus a Harley. Maybe there has been some sort of party here.

Sylvia's dog settles down and stops barking. After about two minutes of nobody answering the door, I take it upon myself to pound on it, alternating between my fist and my knuckles.

Finally, I hear footsteps approaching.

The front door opens and standing before us is a sixty-something looking man of average height who wears a tweed jacket complete with leather elbow patches, an itchy-looking wool sweater and corduroy slacks and leather loafers. He has salt and pepper colored, straight brown hair.

"Hello. Can I help you?" he asks with great poise. He kind of reminds me of a couple of professors I had in business school.

Scott, from what I am gathering, is not good for much. So I decide to take the lead and do the talking.

"We are friends with Sylvia who lives across the street and–"

"I'm her boyfriend," Scott says, interrupting me. I figure he is still trying to assert some sort of ownership over her. "And well, she never came home last night."

This smarmy old man with a slightly greenish complexion touches his chin in thought. "Are you speaking about the lovely young woman that lives across the street?"

"Yeah," Scott replies.

"Sylvia Henderson?" the old man asks.

I nod affirmatively.

"Well, isn't this a coincidence. I mean what a small world? Well, I should not be saying that because this is a small town after all. But as a matter of fact Sylvia is a client of mine."

I don't like the way this guy is using the word "client." For one, because Sylvia happens to be a client of mine and we are about to enter an exclusive partnership. For a moment I wonder if she is cutting deals with some local agent on the sly. But then again, I'm not thinking straight. Ever since I got that desperate text from Sylvia I have not been myself.

"Can you clarify what you mean by *client*?" I ask.

"Listen, this is a dog-friendly home. Why don't the two of you step inside. From my personal and professional perspective I sense we have a crisis on our hands."

"You can say that again," Scott says.

We go inside the entry and the first thing I take note of – which sends off internal alarms – is the fact the house is completely barren of furniture.

"Excuse the lack of, well creature comforts, as the new renter of this home has yet to receive their delivery of furniture. So really there is no place to sit down. Would the doggy like some treats?"

"No thanks," Scott says. "Sylvia has her on a special anti-allergy diet."

"So . . ." I say, interrupting the petty small-talk, "you were saying she's your client." I truly want to get down to business with this pseudo-intellectual.

"Yes, I am her psychiatrist. Pleasure to meet you. I am Dr. Meadows."

We introduce ourselves and then I jump right in. "We happened upon your little letter to Sylvia. I have never heard of people like you coming to their patients home to drop off post."

His answer is slow and deliberate. "I take a special interest in anybody who steps through my office door. I am proactive and community-oriented. My goal is to help people become stabilized as quickly as possible. And I guess if that means I do a few things off the books, well so be it. Report me if you wish. I mean well."

Right away I'm not getting a good impression from this psychiatrist. Something simply doesn't feel right.

"We came here to ask if you have seen Sylvia, but I find it to be a little odd that you are here in this house across the street from hers."

"Maybe it isn't so strange. You see I am kind of multi-tasking today. I dropped off the letter for Sylvia and my good friend from the gym happens to live across the street so I thought since I was out of the office I would drop by and say hello to him."

"Okay, so where is your *good friend from the gym*?" I ask. I am getting a knot in my stomach from the pompous attitude of this elder.

"He is upstairs with another friend of ours."

This shrink doesn't clarify a single thing he says.

"Okay then, are they coming down soon? I would like to ask them about Sylvia."

"I can go upstairs and get them if you'd like."

"What the hell are they doing up there anyway if you are down here?" I feel I am onto something. But I have no idea what it is. All I know is that this house is stuffy, like the central heating has been cranked up too high.

"Do you want me to go up there and get them or not?" he asks.

"Please do," Scott says. I hate it when he butts in. I am a skilled negotiator. I am comfortable in tense situations. As I often sit at round tables with showbusiness sharks in order to close deals. I don't ever lose my cool. Nor do I act overly nice.

"Just one moment please," Dr. Meadows says. He turns, heads up the creaky steps to an upstairs hallway. I can hear some muffled distant talk. A door closes and we wait.

"That man does not sit right with me," I say quietly to Scott.

"What do you mean?" he whispers back.

"I have a good sense of people. And I think this one has a screw loose. Like I said, I've never heard of any kind of doctor leaving a little love letter in the mailbox of a patient."

"Little love letter? You see it that way?"

"You bet your fucking ass I see it that way."

Now, Scott takes a deep breath. I can tell his inner workings have been activated by the way he now juts his chest. He seems to be transferring his sexual jealousy from me to Dr. Meadows.

"Well, fuck him," Scott says.

The minutes drag on. I check the time on my cellphone and about five minutes have already passed.

Scott whispers again, "What did the guy do? Go take a crap?"

"Not very hospitable to just keep us waiting. Come on," I say, and head for the stairway. "Follow me."

"You want us to just go up there. Is that polite?"

"Who cares about polite? He has left us down here for far too long. Something fucked up is happening here."

It is then that I show Scott that I am packing. I have owned a gun since I was thirty years old and was mugged right in front of my then, Greenwich Village townhouse. Luckily they didn't do anything but ruff me up and take my wallet. After that I frequented the Westside Rifle and Pistol Range store on West Twentieth street. For over a decade I have had a permit to carry my trusted Springfield XD-S for a moment just like this.

Scott's eyes widen when he sees the silver pistol.

"What the fuck?" he whispers.

"Come on, Scott. Lets do this."

"Do what?"

"I don't know. But let's find out."

Scott tugs at the dog's leash and follows me up the steps.

"Shhh . . . be as quiet as you can?" I say.

I reach the top of the stairs. Scott follows close behind. We are in a dark hallway without a single framed picture on the wall. There are at least four closed doors.

So far, we have been as quiet as we can. And then the dog starts to bark and our cover is blown. They now know we have taken it upon ourselves to walk upstairs. This time the dog is freaking out. She growls, snarls and barks at an ear-splitting volume.

"I have never seen Sweetie act this way," Scott says in a hushed voice.

"Dogs are highly intuitive," I say.

"I guess."

I reach for the first door I see and open it. I peek inside with my hand gripping my holstered gun. Inside it is just an empty room with the curtains drawn. I shut the door. I try the next door. I open it and this room has such thick curtains that it is almost pitch black inside. I take out my phone and quickly switch it to flashlight mode. I shine the light on each corner of the room. Another empty room. Only two more to go. I try the next door. This door is locked. Bingo. I pound on the door, "Listen Mr. Meadows, sorry I mean Dr. Meadows, we have been waiting downstairs for a long time. Is everything okay?"

I try the door again. I knock some more.

"You are aware that it isn't polite to keep your guests waiting," I say, and give Scott a wink. Scott looks far more nervous than me. But then again he doesn't have a gun.

Finally there is an answer. "Be right out. Sorry, lost track of time. Just a sec."

It is the voice of Dr. Meadows all right. And then I detect another voice. The dog doesn't stop barking and tugging at her leash. My heart is racing. The door opens and I unlatch my gun from its holster. I am not entirely sure what sort of situation we are in. And I don't want it to escalate unnecessarily.

"That dog is pretty crazy," Dr. Meadows says standing in the doorway.

"She only barks when she sees Sylvia," Scott chimes in.

"Well then your dog is right on the button. Because she's here."

I push Dr. Meadows aside and charge into the room. Another empty room. Darkened by the closed curtain. A single lightbulb flickering above. A tall, chiseled guy is standing next to Sylvia. He presses a gun to her temple. The leather-clad guy is there too. He is also armed. Scott comes in with the dog like this is a family get-together. His face goes pale.

I withdraw my gun and hold it at my side.

I notice then the mattress on the floor.

"Are you okay?" I ask Sylvia.

"Tell him," the chiseled guy tells her.

"I'm– I'm okay," she says, voice quivering.

"I don't know what is happening here," I say, "but you men had better get ahold of yourselves. You know police hounds have even better noses than Sylvia's dog. Once they start sniffing around they are going to find all of us in a hot minute. Just let her go. And I will get her out of here. And after that the three of you can go to hell."

"Please, Hank. These are very dangerous men," Sylvia says.

"Is this guy over here in the tweed jacket even your psychiatrist?" I ask her.

"He was. I mean I went to his office once."

"If I had known you before this past weekend I would have warned you off going. Some of them are far more fucked up than the people who come to them for help." I turn to Dr Meadows. "What have you been doing doc, dropping your own pharmaceutical bullshit?"

"You are not understanding what is happening here," he replies.

"Well then, you had better tell me. But make it quick," I reply, the hand on my gun is growing damp.

"We found Sylvia in her home, and she had taken an overdose. She recovered and we brought her here where she would be safe."

"What the fuck? And you didn't take her to the ER?" I say.

"I am a doctor. All she needed was some charcoal pills and she did okay."

"So you take her from her own home and put a gun to her head?"

"Well, the reason there is a gun to her head is because my little helpers here are taking this a little too far."

"Your helpers? What the fuck?" I say.

"I hired them to help me control Sylvia. You see she is acting out in dangerous ways that are at odds with her physical and mental safety. It didn't help that the two of you ingested illicit drugs in New York City. She has told us everything. I believe that is what has triggered her episode."

"Sylvia. Is any of this true?" I ask.

"Tell him," the GQ guy says, as he moves the barrel of the gun to her cheek.

"No, I'm not crazy. These men, they are the ones who are out of their minds."

Sweetie starts barking again. This time she is showing her fangs. Dr. Meadows shuts the door and so the dog's continued barking banks off the walls.

"I should shut that dog up," the biker guy says.

"Please, no," Sylvia says.

Dr. Meadows begins to pet the dog. The dog calms down and becomes quiet.

"Put the gun down, Phil," Leather Man says in his guttural voice to the guy named Phil.

Phil keeps the gun on Sylvia. "And what if I say no?"

"I would not recommend that," Dr. Meadows says calmly.

"Put the gun down and hand Sylvia over to my buddy over here."

Phil suddenly doesn't seem very macho any more. He has been rendered impotent and the sparkle seems to leave his eyes. His gun hand is visibly shaking. Sylvia is also shaking, and clearly trying to hold back her tears.

"You paid me to do this job, Dr. Meadows. I did what you wanted. I brought her here," Phil says.

"But you went far beyond the call of duty by kidnapping her," Dr. Meadows says. "That is not what I hired you to do."

"You hired him?"

"Yes, to rent this house and put Sylvia under surveillance."

Dr. Meadows clenches his teeth and I can see veins protrude upon his forehead. Yet he somehow manages to keep his cool.

"Phil, put the gun down and get out of here?"

Scott, from what I can tell, is also hot under the collar. He looks ready to spring into action. And I suppose he would if it weren't for the presence of the guns.

A gun goes off. The silencer muffles most of its sound. The Leather Man is thrust backward from the impact of the bullet. He grips his shoulder. His jacket is torn, blood gushing from it.

"Sonofabitch," the Leather Man says, barely able to hold his gun up.

Having been the one who shot Leather Man, Phil is now pressing the barrel of his gun to Sylvia's mouth.

I now have my gun trained on Phil and am ready to take the shot. But I'm not a very experienced marksman. I can't be sure my bullet won't hit Sylvia.

That's when the dog starts barking again. Scott crouches down and unleashes Sweetie, who leaps towards Sylvia. Scott takes the loose leash in hand and quickly takes hold of Dr. Meadows, overpowering him by wrapping the leash around his neck. The Leather Man is still incapacitated from the pain of having been shot in the shoulder.

Dr. Meadows manages to shout out, "Kill them all!" before his windpipe is cut off from the leash.

The dog is trying to jump into Sylvia's arms. Leather Man seems to only have a surface wound and with his good hand holding the gun, pops off a shot at Phil.

It hits him just below his heart. Phil drops his gun,

and takes hold of his chest which is now profusely gushing blood.

Dr. Meadows surprises me with his physical prowess as he elbows backwards into Scott's ribs and steps down on Scott's foot, pounding his fist into his groin.

Scott loses his grip on the leash around Dr. Meadows's neck and the psychiatrist breaks free and makes a leap for Phil's gun which has dropped onto the floor.

Sylvia manages to stoop down and snatch the gun away just in time.

She is standing firm with the blood-soaked gun in hand. She alternates between pointing the gun at the psychiatrist and the Leather Man, who is in turn, ready to fire at her.

"Don't even fucking think about pulling that trigger," Dr. Meadows says, while on his hands and his knees in a puddle of blood.

CHAPTER FORTY-TWO

SYLVIA

The man dressed all in leather thinks I'm kidding.

"Listen lady," he says, "I don't mean you any harm. I was just hired to come get you. I don't have a beef with you. And Phil over there is the one who fucked up everything."

"Don't speak. Just drop the gun," I say.

"I can't do that. I ain't going back to the pen."

"I came to get the lady and now all this shit has gone down I really don't know what you want me to do. Killing her was never part of the deal. You just told me you wanted me to keep her in this fucking house."

"Yes, not tie her up. And Now I order you to kill everyone!" Dr. Meadows shouts.

The wounded man seems to be listening to his boss again. He squints his eyes at me like a hungry bear as I pull the trigger. The bullet catches him in the throat. He begins to choke. He drops his gun and grips his neck as blood seeps between his fingers.

Phil manages to slither in his own pool of blood over to me and grab me by the leg to try and pull me down.

"You did this to me."

He tugs at me and I slip on his blood and fall to the floor.

He starts choking me, wearing an ecstatic expression as though he is getting a thrill out of cutting off my airway. I have dropped the gun and it is now submerged in blood.

I hear another shot. This time it is Hank who has shot Phil. But it does not stop him. He is still on top of me, riding me, choking me. I somehow manage to take hold of my slippery gun and press it to his heart and shoot. Suddenly I have all his dead weight on me. Suffocating me. Hank and Scott pull him off me and clumsily help me to my feet. I can now see that the hulk in leather is no longer breathing. Phil is most certainly dead. His eyes are wide and staring blankly at eternity.

Yet someone is missing.

Dr. Meadows has left the building.

Hank heads out of the room in pursuit of him.

I hurry to the window and peek through the curtains and see Dr. Meadows rushing to get into his car. He starts the engine and drives off. He is halfway up the block by the time Hank steps out to the front yard.

I wonder if Hank rented a car when he came into town. But now I can only guess he took an Uber to my place. He has no way of pursuing Dr. Meadows.

I stop my dog from licking the blood on the floor, "Come on Sweetie, lets get out of here."

Scott and I leave the two limp, lifeless bodies in the room.

I know now that I will have to, as soon as I can, move out of this block. I will never be able to live across the street from this house of horror. Every time I look out my bay windows I will think of the terror that has just taken place here.

As we step outside, I realize what a blood-drenched sight we must be to see. I can tell by the startled looks on the faces in the cars passing when they get a look at us. I know it won't be long before the police show up whether we call 911 or not.

One of us has to call the cops. Hank takes on that duty.

The cops will be arriving shortly. It won't take them long to track Dr Meadows down. A man who is well-known within the community he lives cannot be hard to find. He won't be able to return to his office or his home. All he can do now is drive.

I can hear the sirens now, instantly reminding me of what came before. As though my life is a song on repeat.

CHAPTER FORTY-THREE

ANNE

I watch as my daughter once again is questioned by the police. She is sitting at her dining room table inside her home opposite a detective, observed by two cops. While that fine catch of a man named Hank stands around looking like all he has on his mind are the slick expensive lawyers he is surely planning to hire. This is the last thing he needs to deal with. No media mogul wants to be engulfed in scandal. And then there is Scott, who I could tell was in shock. Poor guy, he has been so patiently courting Sylvia. Some men just never give up.

My husband Harold, who has just arrived at her house, was that way with me once upon a time. Harold must have invited me out on at least a dozen dates until I succumbed and accepted his offer of dinner and a movie. He is not even allowed to hug blood-soaked Sylvia and he begins to sob. Mostly with relief and gratitude that his daughter has made it through another harrowing incident that might have killed her.

He now knows his Sylvia and the others are all suspects in a murder investigation. They are driven to the police station with their hands bagged and in handcuffs. At the police station the bags are removed, and their clothing is photographed, nails scraped, clothing removed and they are given baggy clothing to change into. Then they are allowed to shower.

Next, they are taken to an audio and visually recorded interview room where I watch as they have their mouths swabbed. Everyone except Sylvia who they already have on file from what happened with her and Will a year ago. They have their fingerprints taken. Except Sylvia who they already have on file to match against any found at Phil's house.

CSI is meanwhile scouring the scene of the crime with a video camera, taking photographs and swabbing things for DNA analysis.

Hank arranges for the best local lawyers to be brought in.

Dr. Meadows' odd and self-incriminating letter is used as evidence to help their case and to prove he had ill will against Sylvia.

They are given bail after forty-eight hours, because at last, the police believe they are all telling the truth.

Yet, as my husband learns the details of what has transpired over the last few weeks he appears to become even more visibly concerned. Any father would. He now knows all about Dr. Meadows. Harold regrets ever advising she see that cracked psychiatrist. And he seems more exacerbated when he learns that the berserk doctor is still at large.

When the police drive Sylvia back to her home Harold is there waiting for her.

"Listen, honey," Harold says to Sylvia, as he takes her hands into his, "you can stay with me until they find that maniac. It's not safe for you to stay here."

"Mr. Henderson," the detective sitting beside Sylvia says, "we will have two squad cars keeping a watch on your daughter's home until we find the perpetrator."

"Just have them park in front of my house. Honey, I insist," Harold says.

"If you don't mind my butting in Mr. Henderson," Hank says, "I would like to bring her on my private jet and get her out of town. She will be safer with me in New York. My building has unmatched security."

"That is a bit selfish of you," Scott says. "Why don't we compromise, and I will just stay here with her in her own home where she will be most comfortable."

These are the three men in my Sylvia's life. They are surely putting her in a quandary.

Does she want to go back to her childhood home so that her father can fry her favorite pancakes and sausage links in the morning? Does she want Hank to whisk her away and hide her like Rapunzel in his high-rise? Or does she want Scott to watch over her, so that the two of them can work things out?

I wish I could help her decide. But she can't hear my voice, so she is unable to heed it. All I can do is pray she makes the right choice and hope it works out for her.

She wraps her arms around herself as if to feel warmer and inhales. She looks up and I wonder if she can feel my presence.

CHAPTER FORTY-FOUR

SIX MONTHS LATER

HANK

I'm sure that Scott is still morose knowing that Sylvia has chosen me over him. And I can only hope he doesn't see it as the materialistic choice. I hope her dad does not see it that way either. What I've learned about Sylvia over these last few months is that she is not what Madonna would have labeled a "Material Girl." I just think some women in the end just want a man to help her feel safe. And with my funds I can offer her protection beyond what the police can. Besides, the protection they offered was solely for Grand Rapids and the surrounding areas and now she lives in my Union Square loft with me.

It's springtime in the city. And there is renewed energy in the air.

Sylvia has spent many a sleepless night with me. Shortly after the incident and after all the questioning was through and we were each cleared of any wrongdoing by the police, she broke it to Scott. She told him that she had made her choice to live with me. He didn't take it well.

I stayed in her home and helped her make all the

many arrangements to get her the hell out of that town which had brought her so much grief.

With the help of Angelique, we secured a moving company, and a realtor that would sell her house at a decent price, so that she could recoup her initial investment.

I could tell Sylvia had mixed feelings about leaving her home. Yet the negative memories were too intense. This was where she had once been married to a man who had almost murdered her. Not to mention it was across the street from where multiple acts of violence, that would give anyone nightmares, had occurred. I am still feeling the effect of having shot Phil. The image of that heavyset man in leather taking his last gasp while flopped down like a lampooned whale in his own blood still haunts me and probably always will.

Scott stopped by those first few following days while I stayed on at her house. He demanded to see her, to talk to her, to reason with her, to win her back, to convince her to stay in Grand Rapids, to marry him and yes give his a child. I have never seen such a desperate, lovelorn man. He would often bring her to tears. I allowed them their space yet would never leave the house as they argued, and cried, and argued again. When he struck her during one such visit I stormed into the living room and demanded he leave her house immediately. That was when he struck me. A firm fist directly into my face. He had real gusto backing up that blow. But I was no pushover and I jabbed him back in the ribs. He then punched me again, this time in the solar plexus. While gasping for air, I swiped my feet under him, knocking him off his. Then I got on top of him. And with my knees, pinned him down while Sylvia yelled, "Stop!"

Scott is bigger than me, but obviously not as used

to fighting as me. He resisted my weight vigorously until he toppled me over. This time he got on top of me. And he was not just trying to contain me. He was in an all out jealous rage.

That is when I reached for the switchblade attached to my belt and pressed the edge to his throat.

"Get off me now or I will cut you," I said.

Scott froze.

"Get up off of him," Sylvia demanded of Scott.

Scott stood, slowly.

"I can't believe you just fucking did this to me," he said, with agony in his voice.

"No, Scott, I have done nothing wrong. I have just changed. I am sorry I think I love Hank," she said.

***

And as I sit here in my loft, at my desk, trying to focus on my business affairs, I can still picture her face that afternoon. Her eyes puffy from the crying. Her hand shaking.

This is why it's so beneficial for her to now be living with me here in New York. It's me and her now. And Scott is simply not stable anymore. I believe I am best for her now and I am sorry feelings had to get hurt.

Her house was not easy to flip. People knew one man had been shot by Sylvia there. So we dropped the price and closed on the property. As for Scott, he learned his lesson. Sylvia and I filed a restraining order against him and that should stop him from coming anywhere near either of us any time soon.

Sylvia has been remarkably resilient. She loves to explore the city and is not afraid to do so on her own, while I work. We have attended Broadway shows –

musicals are her favorite. We have frequented the Met, the Guggenheim, and we have dined from Koreatown to Chinatown and we have walked along the South Street Seaport and taken in gallery shows in Chelsea and Soho. She has become amazingly fashion-forward. She fits right in.

In these short few months, she has become sassy. She has clipped her hair into a bob and she now looks positively post-mod and she would not look out of place on the catwalk. She may not have made any new friends of her own. But that's okay. My friends just love her. And she loves them back. As far as our business deal is concerned, well let's just say it's on hold for now. It doesn't feel right to me to exploit her story at this time. Perhaps later, when the dust settles.

As for her fear of Dr. Meadows, well that fear has been quelled as well. He had been missing for at least a month until his car collided with a Mack truck carrying fireworks on the M 21. The truck driver survived the explosive crash. But the psychiatrist's car went up in flames. His vehicle was totaled and the only remains of the man that were salvaged in the wreckage was his lower jaw. The teeth matched his DNA and his dental records.

The doctor was torched, incinerated, cremated by karmic fate. And the world is that much better for it.

CHAPTER FORTY-FIVE

SYLVIA

Scott will never speak to me again. After all, my new boyfriend placed a switchblade against his throat in self-defense. I also stand by my difficult decision to take out a restraining order against him. And I am glad I managed to get the hell out of Michigan.

I love the anonymity that I have here in Manhattan. Nobody knows about me here. This past year in Grand Rapids has been very hard on me. Talk about getting the cold-eye from strangers. I would often wear hats and sunglasses to avoid those judgmental glares. And I resented that terribly and even spoke to Hank about suing the papers for what they have written about me. Many still believe what I did was not in self-defense. He told me to take it in my stride and reminded me that I would soon live far away from the local bad press. He also reminded me that my national press was predominantly positive and that is why he initially took such a great interest in me.

Now I am free. And Hank is good to me. Really he is. And it is not just that he is generous with me. He is, but it is so much more than that. He is very in-tune with my moods. Sometimes I just want to be left alone to roam the sights and the sounds of the city. I love to go to Times Square at night and getting lost in the crowd of tourists under all those vibrant video billboards and lights imagining my own image up on a video screen like a Times Square Goddess. He has been honest with me and has told me that after the bloodbath at the house across the street from mine my already not very squeaky-clean image has been further tarnished and it'll take a while to recoup.

This very evening I decide to have coffee at a Starbucks on 42nd street and Broadway. I sit and look out the window at the crowds and I once again think back to the Grand Rapids police investigation sting. They really went to town on my behalf. They researched the Leather Man, AKA Tommy K – a hardened criminal who had been in prison for breaking and entering and attempted manslaughter during a foiled attempt at kidnapping a teen daughter of a local, wealthy resident. And then there was Phil – AKA Phil Lowes who turned out to be a petty thief and a freelance gun-for-hire who had also been in the pen. Unfortunately, they were not able to find any other abettors connected to my abduction. Dr. Meadows, they discovered, had a tainted record as a doctor and his license to practice psychotherapy had once been under suspension and review because he had taken an inappropriately personal interest in another female patient and had placed her in an empty apartment he owned as a favor.

She claimed that he would visit her there and practice mind control on her which has left her psychologically and emotionally damaged. She did assure the authorities that he did not molest her in any way. And there was no evidence that he did. As for the mind control claim, it was her word against his and Dr. Meadows stated on the record to the review panel that he was only trying to save her from homelessness. And that his visits were solely therapeutic. And so he was somehow able to practice again.

And that is really hard for me to take. I just at least want to know why that sicko doctor had it in for me so bad.

They went into his records and have found no other indiscretions besides me and that woman. I considered contacting her but Hank advised me to move on. And I realized it is best I do. Turns out Dr. Meadows had been one of the most in-demand psychiatrists in West Michigan. All that I really learned is that he studied and did his internship right here at Columbia. At my request – to be sure he was dead – I asked the cops to show me a full color photo of what was left of his jaw and teeth. Some of his teeth were crowned in gold and others in silver. They had found his dental records and it all matched up. I don't mean to be morbid but I am happy he suffered a painful death.

I can only imagine that when he slammed the breaks and his car became wedged under that Mack truck that his face must have slammed so hard against the steering wheel that it broke his jaw. The cops told me that his airbags never inflated.

After my cup of coffee I cross the street and have Sushi. I am happy to sit alone. Though I have not been sleeping well lately, I feel like I live in a bubble of Hank's adoration. He really does put me on a pedestal. I don't think we have had a single meal at home. It always has to be a night of dining out at places that are shockingly expensive. Sometimes, when I look at the menus and see the prices I almost gasp.

The lovemaking has been stimulating. We have

learned so much about each other's bodies. Hank is not a tall man. Maybe five foot eight-and-a-half. But he's compact and fit. And he's a real good lover. Always aware of my needs. I always am the one who climaxes first. Sometimes he pulls me by the legs to the edge of the bed and he gets on his knees and buries his face between my legs.

When I arrive back at the loft, Hank is barefoot and dressed in Bermuda shorts and a simple white T-shirt. He is in bed with his laptop on his knees as he speaks into his smartphone headset. He smiles when he sees me. He is talking numbers and figures and percentages of deals I am not privy to.

Sweetie runs to me and I pick her up and hold her in my arms. She is a city dog now and has been adapting well to her new surroundings, except it is a bit of a chore to remember to take her for quick walks around the block three times a day so that she can go do a number one or two. It was so much easier when I had my house in Grand Rapids and she could come and go as she pleased through her doggy door. Mornings, I take her right across the street to the Union Square dog run and let her go wild without her leash. She loves other dogs and though I am a bit wary of dog parks she has not had any issues with any of the other hounds.

What I guess I am saying is that life is good. And I truly never thought it would be again.

Correction, life is good but not perfect.

I hate living so far from my father. It just doesn't feel right that he should be the only family member living in Grand Rapids. I know he is lonely out there without me – his only child. Now he has lost my mother and me. I have mentioned this with Hank and he has offered to fly my father out to New York City in his private jet. Hank has also arranged to have a private town car pick up my father at the airport.

On the night of my father's arrival Hank has convinced me to remain at home and relax. I wanted to be there at LaGuardia to greet my father but Hank assures me that my father will be fine.

When my father walks into Hank's loft I am overflowing with conflicting feelings. I feel guilty for having left my father and I want so much to make it up to him. There are bags under his eyes, and he looks older and thinner than the last time I saw him. His cheeks seem more hollow.

"Dad, you have to eat more for God's sake," I say as we hug.

"I was on a the Mediterranean diet and started losing so much weight I went off it. Now I eat like a pig and cannot gain it back," my father says.

Hank and my father shake hands.

"Great to see you, Mr. Henderson," Hank says.

"Thanks so much for flying me out."

"Don't even mention it. Can I get you a drink. Perhaps some wine?"

"Sure, why the hell not."

"I'll have some too, honey," I say, and my father takes note of my endearment towards Hank.

"Red or white, Mr. Henderson?"

"Please call me Harold. And I will have red, thank you."

"Okay, Harold. I have been talking it over with Sylvia and we would like to offer to make arrangements for you to move to New York City. That way the two of you can be close to each other."

"Oh, man, that's quite an offer."

"It was my idea, Dad," I say, sitting next to my father on the white leather couch.

"It sounds like far too much trouble on my accord. I'm quite happy in my quiet little house. I'm not sure if I am cut out for big city life."

"Why not?" I ask my father.

"Well, I know my way around Grand Rapids. The grocery store is just a few blocks from me."

"Mr. Henderson . . . I mean Harold, I think you will find Manhattan to be the most convenient place in the world."

"So many people everywhere. And the buildings block the sun. I really don't know."

"Really, think about it Dad. You saw how fast Hank made all the arrangements for me. And he can do the same for you. He used to be in real estate before he started his media company."

Hank hands my father his glass of red wine.

"Thank you kind sir. I will think on it. But if I do decide to relocate, it won't be because I want to live in New York. It will be so I can be near you, Sylvia. Hank, you must know that Sylvia means everything to me."

"Well, she's my world now also. So we have that in common."

Hank clinks my dad's glass then mine and we take a sip of our drinks.

My father is set up in a guest room in Hank's loft. I have made his bed with fresh sheets and there is a fifty-inch flat screen TV in his room as well as his own private bathroom. There is a part of me that would love for my father to stay right here and live with Hank and me in this loft. That way I could look after my father who may be only fifty-nine, but lately – from all the stress I have caused him – has been looking like he is pushing seventy.

How much longer will I have him in my life? I have no way of knowing.

Hank and I prepare for bed, and we settle in for a movie and I nod off but that is only because I have been trying to catch up on my sleep. Lately, it seems – perhaps due to incessant worrying – I haven't been getting much at all. Instead, I take cat-naps during the day.

When I wake up from my fitful light sleep of an hour, the bedroom is dark and only Sweetie is at the foot of the bed, Hank is not there. I lie there a while then get up to make myself a midnight snack to fuel what is surely going to be another bout of insomnia. I figure Hank is in the kitchen snacking again. He is a night eater too, yet he never gains weight. I envy him that. He remains svelte despite his enormous appetite for gourmet foods.

Walking down the hall I hear hushed voices inside the guest room where my dad should be sleeping. It sounds like Hank and my dad are talking privately. Isn't that the sweetest thing!

"Sylvia has been having a hard time with her sleep. She is up most of the night," Hank says.

"Has she tried sleeping pills?" my dad asks.

"No, she refuses to take them, but have tried pretty much everything else. Nothing seems to work. She has no trouble falling asleep but then she wakes up again. I find her in the living room, snacking, reading, or watching TV, sometimes till 4 a.m."

"That is something to keep an eye on."

"Look, I don't want to keep you up for too long. But I do think it would be best if you move here to New York. After all that has happened to her she could do with having you around. I try but I cannot give her all of the emotional support she needs. In fact I have researched it, and if this continues, I mean if she simply does not sleep, I read online that it can be dangerous for her brain chemistry. I have suggested sleeping aids but Sylvia won't hear of it. I have consulted with a doctor over the phone and she told me to contact her if and when she stops sleeping altogether."

"And then what?"

"I could take her to a highly recommended facility in Valhalla that has a state of the art sleep clinic. I am sure they have medications that can sedate her so that she can go to and stay asleep for the entire night."

"I'm glad I came out here. I was not aware of any of this."

"She needs you."

"You are a good man, Hank."

I simply cannot believe they are talking about me in this manner. Like I am a danger to myself. Okay, so I have not been getting a full night of sleep. But there are plenty of very successful people who survive on only four hours a night. One thing for damn sure is that I will not allow them to send me to what Hank is referring to as a "sleep clinic" but is most probably an outlet of a looney bin. Now I understand why Hank kept dropping hints at having my father visit. I get it. I have figured this out. They figure if my father signs the papers then they can have me admitted to a psychiatric hospital.

I burst into the guest room.

"What the hell is going on in here!" I say at the top of my voice. "I never thought the two of you would be best buddies."

"Sylvia," my father says. He sitting up in the bed, Hank in his boxers and his favorite black bathrobe seated on a chair.

"We have just been chatting," Hank says.

"About what?"

"Just shooting the shit," Hank says.

"My ears have been turning green because you both were clearly talking about me."

"You heard us?" Dad asks. He looks so tired.

"The walls in this loft are thin," I say.

"Okay, we have nothing to hide," Hank says. "I was telling your father about your insomnia."

"I heard everything and if you think you are going to send me to some mental institution all because I have a little trouble sleeping your are dead wrong."

"I suggested to your father that is what we might try if your problem persists. And Valhalla is not an *institution*. It is a clinic that covers the gamut from addiction problems to well, all sorts of things . . . sleep included," Hank says.

"By all sorts of things you mean mental breakdowns. I assure you I'm not having a breakdown. I just like staying up at night. Hell, this *is* the city that never sleeps! What do you expect from me?"

CHAPTER FORTY-SIX

WILL

I can see from here that Hank and Sylvia's father wish only the best for her. They just don't understand that they are exacerbating her state of mind by alarming her like that. They should have known better than to discuss her condition in that guest room. They should know she would be up roaming the house and able to overhear them.

I watch as they keep discussing the issue with her for another two hours. They should be trying to relax her so that she can at least attempt to go back to sleep. Soon it is 2 a.m. and by this point Sylvia is quite hyped-up. She is exasperated by the possibility that they would even consider signing her over to a hospital should her condition worsen. The truth is Hank has already attempted to help her with Ambien, melatonin and valerian pills as well as valium, weed, wine and everything under the sun to calm her so that she gets a proper eight or nine hours of sleep. I believe she is traumatized, not only by what she has done to me but also for the things she saw in that house across the street from her former home.

Now, she is really upset. So much so that she is yelling at her father. She says she wishes he had not come to visit her. She claims they are both just trying to humiliate her. She turns her newfound wrath on Hank, saying that now that she lives under his roof he is trying to control her thoughts like Dr. Meadows was probably planning to do. I am sure the next door tenants in that condo on 14th street can hear her carrying on. She says she simply can no longer handle the men in her life. She yells out that she wishes she were a lesbian. Because maybe a woman would not want to dominate her. To keep her. She claims that neither of them is aware but she has been catching her ZZ's throughout the day and that the whole REM sleep thing is a hoax and a conspiracy.

It is clear to the two of them that Sylvia has become unhinged. She won't settle down, no matter how they try to calm her. They even try to change the subject. Yet they still refuse to promise that she won't need to go somewhere to get her sleep regulated. At one point Hank gives a secret signal to Sylvia's father to keep talking to her, while he slips into his office, where he makes a phone call. He is calling a crisis hotline and he is asking for help. They say over the phone that they have twenty-four-seven crisis counselors that do make home visits if needed. They tell Hank they can have two of them visit his loft within the hour. He reluctantly agrees.

Ironically, Sylvia settles down, and is restfully sitting on the living room couch when Hank comes back into the room. Her father has been successful in ramping down her state of mind. Yet she still doesn't want to go to bed. She says she wants to sleep on the couch. And a whole production is made where they bring her sheets, pillows and a comforter, as well as placing Sweetie at her feet. Yet, it is clear she is never gong to actually sleep. She has been far too riled-up by the confrontation. She begins to cry. And it is while she is crying when they hear the intercom sound.

Hank answers and buzzes their visitors inside.

When he opens the door, two middle-aged men dressed in drab tones enter the loft. One is bald, the other grey. Both are clean-shaven and dressed business-causal. With hushed voices they come into the living room where Sylvia is under the covers talking to her father.

"Who are these people?" Sylvia asks.

And from there on things get less and less civil. Sylvia simply cannot accept the fact that Hank would betray her and bring two crisis team members to his loft at 3 a.m. She insists she is ready to go to sleep and that everyone is just overreacting. The team members sit on the other leather couches across from her. They try asking her some simple questions. Like how and when did her insomnia start.

She refuses to talk to them. She gets up off the couch and says she is going to take Sweetie for a night walk. And one of the counselors suggests that this is not a good idea. He suggests she remain in a "controlled" environment. Hank tries to stop her. She pushes him away and starts looking for the dog's leash. She is unable to find it because Hank has managed to hide it somewhere she won't discover it.

She ignores the men and she finds the remote and switches on Pandora radio. She scrolls to her favorite music channel. The song *Sunday Morning* by Maroon 5 comes on and she just starts dancing all by herself as though she couldn't care less who is observing her, or what assessment they are making of her behavior. And that is when they leave the room to discuss things privately. The bald team member makes a call. She continues dancing. A bit suggestively this time. She is a sensual sight to see. She is smiling. Laughing. She even holds up Sweetie and dances with her dog in her arms.

Only when the police arrive does that smile leave her face.

The last words she utters as she is taken away are, "Sweetie! Please don't take me away from Sweetie!"

CHAPTER FORTY-SEVEN

SYLVIA

I have been in the clinic for a couple of days and I have to say it is not half bad. Outside, on the grounds, patients throw frisbees in the warm spring air. I really don't even know what they have given me here but it sure got my sleep regulated quick. They have dosed me up pretty good. Most of the in-patients that I have met are wealthy twenty-somethings with substance abuse problems. Mostly they just complain about not being able to use their cellphones. I have met a beautiful woman roughly my age whose husband had her admitted because she had an affair. She insists there is nothing wrong with her and she has been using the hall phone to speak to her lawyer. She often sits on the floor talking on it for so long that the nurses tell her that she has to free up the line so that other's can make calls. There is a guy with long straight hair who they allow to play his acoustic guitar. He can't have his guitar in his room because it has steel strings and that goes against a Valhalla policy since he could use the strings to slit his wrists or hang himself. Usually, a nurse brings him his guitar in the evening and he sings for those of us that wish to listen. He really is quite good. He sings songs by

James Taylor and Dave Mathews and his voice has a soothing effect on me.

I feel like I am in a resort.

My father, has been staying on at Hank's loft and the two of them have visited me every day, bringing with them health food stacks. They tell me that now that my sleeping disorder has been sorted out I should be let out within a day or so.

Today is my fourth day here, and the first that I will see an actual doctor. So far I have only spoken with physician assistants. They are called "PAs" here.

A young, curvy Latina nurse leads me to an office with a couch, a desk and a window facing the sprawling grounds outside. I sit down and wait while listening to the Kenny G music in the room.

The doctor arrives shortly thereafter. He is a pudgy little man that reminds me of Danny DeVito. He introduces himself as Dr. Katz and he sits down and switches on his laptop.

"How has your visit with us at Valhalla gone so far?" he asks.

"It has actually been quite pleasant."

"Do you find your meals to be satisfactory?"

"I had Cornish hen last night that would be good enough to serve at a wedding reception."

"And how is your sleep?"

"I am happy to report that I have been sleeping quite well."

"I see." He keeps looking over his files on his laptop screen. "Well, from what I can see on your patient notes we are pleased with your progress."

"Great, when do you think I can go home?"

"We usually keep people for a seventy-two hour lockdown. And since you are showing signs of remission then . . . I will speak with the front desk about your release."

"Fantastic."

"Yes, Miss. Henderson, things are looking up for you. Do you have any other complaints? Or anything you would like to share."

"The coffee here is not up to par," I say teasingly.

There is a knock at the door.

Dr. Katz gets up and opens it.

From where I am seated I cannot see who is outside. They whisper so I cannot make out what is being said.

Another doctor steps into the office. He has an unsightly patchy beard and wears darkly-shaded glasses. He has a sort of receding chin that makes him look, well to be honest, a little alarming.

"Miss. Henderson, this is our specialist for sleeping disorders, Dr. Ashbury. He is new here at Valhalla."

"Hello Sylvia," he says, sitting down directly across from me. The doctor has a distorting speech impairment. He seems to mumble and he has a strong lisp. "I won't take much of your time. As I unfortunately have a more pressing case to take care of. Dr. Katz, do you mind if I speak with Sylvia alone for a moment?"

"Oh, sure," Dr. Katz says. He gets up and leaves the room promptly, closing the door behind him.

"Sylvia, I have looked over your files . . ." Dr. Ashbury says, as I try not to stare at his deformed chin. His voice is grating on my nerves.

". . . after some observation here at Valhalla, we are happy to inform you that your sleeping disorder is only temporary and most probably not chronic. Probably just stress related. We would like to, if you comply, keep you on a dose of Ambien for a few months or so, and then you can be weened off it if you wish. However, you also do show signs of something else."

Though his words are comforting. It is hard to listen to him. The more I look at him, the more his deformity vexes me.

"Have you ever heard of the term, thought insertion?"

I am still troubled by his unsightly chin and his garbled voice. So much so that it becomes distracting.

"Did you hear what I said, Sylvia? Have you ever heard of the disorder?"

Finally I answer, "No, I have not."

"It is a kind of delusional belief, in which a person can actually think they are having the thoughts of someone other than their self. It makes it difficult for a person to tell the difference between their own thoughts and the thoughts that they believe have been inserted into their minds. Do you understand what I am saying?"

"What does this have to do with me?"

"After conferring with the staff here we believe you are suffering from this disorder."

What he is saying is going right over my head and I certainly cannot see how it applies to me. "Once again, I don't know what you are getting at."

"Let me put it this way, Sylvia, have you ever felt like you are listening to what others are thinking. For instance do you believe you hear the voices of the deceased."

"Of the deceased? You mean like being able to hear dead people?"

"My records show your mother passed away a few years ago. Do you ever think you hear her voice? Or that she is watching over you."

I have had the sensation that she is somehow protecting me but still, I object to this line of reasoning.

"Look, doctor, I don't hear voices of any kind."

"Do you think you know what your boyfriend is thinking? Or your husband, Will?"

"My husband died over a year ago. You know about that?"

"Yes, I have been briefed on the details of that event. And I can imagine it is a sensitive subject for you. Do you ever sense that he is watching over you? Allow me to use a metaphor to strengthen what I am trying to relay to you. Does it feel like your late husband, Will, is a radio host and you are listening to his radio station?"

"You mean like he's a dead DJ? Give me a break."

"What I am saying is that I don't think you truly know why you are here at Valhalla. You believe you are here because you have a sleeping disorder. But actually your case is more severe than that. We have spoken confidentially with your loved ones, and they say that ever since the day you killed your husband – in self-defense we understand – that you have created an elaborate inner world. A world where you hear the voice of your husband, William, as if he is speaking to you from beyond the grave. And that you can also hear the voice of your mother, Anne, who I see succumbed to cancer, and then there are others who you think are speaking through you, a fellow named Scott who you had been dating, and Hank the man who brought you to us. What I am saying Sylvia is that, and I know you will have a hard time processing this, the series of events that you believe have happened to you since you killed your husband, is not in correlation with reality. We have records from a Dr. Meadows here."

Hearing his name spoken by this Dr. Ashbury sends a shockwave through my body. For a moment I feel nauseous and cannot breathe.

"Are you okay, Sylvia? Would you like some

water?"

"Yes, please."

Dr. Ashbury gets up and finds a small bottle of Evian in a fridge. He hands it to me. I open it and after a few sips I am able to respond.

"That guy was a sociopath!" I say, raising my voice.

"Well, we have his records and it shows he was quite concerned about your mental state and tried an intervention because he believed you were acting out by having delusions concerning a man named Phil who had just moved across the street from you. They both tried to restrain you with the help of medical professionals and the whole time you were lost in a fantasy that Phil was "in" on some scheme or "conspiracy" and that one of the nurses on the scene was a "leather man" and that gunfire ensued. When actually this was just our initial attempt to bring you here."

I am confounded by what he is telling me. I don't get any good vibes from him at all.

"Dr. Meadows was a psychopath. His license had once been suspended for fixating on another patient before me, and he was wanted by the Grand Rapids police. He was found dead in a car wreck."

"Is that what you believe?"

"I know so. They found his remains."

As I am speaking and staring at this man's hideous face it begins to dawn on me that there is something spookily eerie about him. The graying hair, the piercing eyes . . .

"What did they find?" Dr. Ashbury asks.

"They found his lower jaw. And it matched his dental records." As I say this it all comes together. I can now see that below this man's beard is a long, thick scar. I get up. I want to run.

"Where are you going, Sylvia?"

"You are Dr. Meadows."

"How would that be possible?"

"You tell me?"

"Lets go through a couple of probable scenarios. Let's say I really am this Dr. Meadows person and I was able to orchestrate my own death. After all, in your mind, I hired those hitmen to abduct you. And so let's say I hired someone to drive my car, an underworld pro who knew how to get in a deadly crash and yet make a quick getaway, and let's say I went to a specialist surgeon and had my lower jaw removed and carefully placed in the wreckage of my car so that my death certificate could be certified. And let's say I took up a new identity so that I could secure your position on this ward. Now tell me Sylvia, would any of this, if you were to now relay it to any doctor here, make them feel that you were sane and ready to leave this hospital any time soon?"

I feel like all my blood is draining from my body. And though I am chilled, my hands are clammy.

What he says is not so far-fetched at all.

"What do you want from me?" I ask, my voice breathy.

"*We* just want you to be well. If that requires keeping you here or transporting you to a facility where you can be properly cared for . . . a place where you can get one-on-one, individual and focused treatment – at my request – then so be it. Even if it is prearranged private housing."

"You are a sick man."

"No Sylvia, you are projecting your illness onto me. It is you who is sick. We can make you well again, but you must decide to help yourself by allowing us."

I can no longer contain my disbelief, my rage. There is no way out of this maze. Except to kill or be killed. He is obviously relentless in his pursuit of –

whatever it is he wants from me – and will never give up. Going as far as to fabricate his own death and take on the identity of another psychiatrist. It is clear he knows people and that he has connections and the means to fund his deviant plans. I will never win until he is no longer breathing.

I rise slowly from my chair to approach him.

He remains seated. I step closer towards him, invading his personal space.

"What are you going to do, Sylvia?"

"I am going to make you wish you *had* died."

"That is interesting. It shows some grandiosity on your part. You actually think that killing me is in your best interest. You know it will only result in you spending your life in a facility far less pleasant than this one or the one I have ready just for you."

"You are not sending me anywhere. I am sending your somewhere."

"And where may I ask, Sylvia, are you sending me?"

"To hell!"

I leap on that man who resembles a monster in a freak show and I grab his throat in my hands. His jaw sounds like it's cracking. The harder and longer I squeeze it feels like whatever is left of his fragile bones is simply crumbling in my grip. His eyes begin to bulge and then he throws his weight on me. He has surprising strength for an old man, and he manages to knock me to the floor.

On top of me now, he is choking me right back. He is a might bit stronger than me.

Finding it hard to breathe, my grip on him loosens as his tightens. His glasses fall off and all I see are the wide, deranged, bloodshot eyes of Dr. Meadows. He has managed to close my windpipe. And I black out for a moment. He is winning this battle.

A beefy looking nurse breaks into the room. And before I black out again he charges at the doctor and takes him in a death grip. He is trying to pry the doctor from me, while Dr Meadows is trying with all his might to shut off my air supply.

CHAPTER FORTY-EIGHT

ANNE

The burley, redhead nurse rips that man from Sylvia's almost lifeless body, then a black nurse bursts into the office and the two of them are finally able to overtake and overpower the old man. Sylvia spits and gasps for air.

From the floor she watches as the redhead pummels Dr. Meadows with punches to the face.

"You sonofabitch. What the hell do you think you are doing to her?" he shouts, while punching so hard that Sylvia can hear the bridge of Dr. Meadows's nose crack and break. And with the next precise punch his jaw comes loose spouting blood. And the lower part of his jaw now just hangs off his face like an appendage.

"Chill out man," the other nurse says, eyes wide to the bloody grotesque sight of the doctor's now mangled face.

"This bastard was trying to choke this woman to death."

"Just stop. You can't be doing this," he says, while watching in horror.

The redhead will not relent. He seems hellbent on killing the doctor. More nurses burst into the office and they all try to stop him from jabbing the doctor's windpipe.

Finally, they are able to topple him to the floor.

The doctor is lying face up. His eyes staring blankly at the ceiling. His face now looking like a crushed, blood-soaked, Halloween death mask. His chest perfectly still.

CHAPTER FORTY-NINE

HANK

I was so happy the day I got Sylvia out of that clinic. I don't mean to be disrespectful towards those who help people in genuine need, but from the cops and what the media reported over the last few days, I have come to the conclusion that the hospital is a mismanaged hellhole. If I thought it was worth it I would sue for outright negligence to the safety of those they are claiming to care for.

The Westchester media reported that Dr. Meadows did in fact stage his own death. A local sting found the driver of his car who fabricated a collision with a Mack truck driver who was also in on the scam. And that sicko doctor did in fact go to an under-the-table and off-the-books surgeon to have a quarter of his lower jaw removed to be placed in his mangled, smoked-out car so that authorities would come to the conclusion that he had suffered a fatal accident. Then this ingenious and resourceful quack managed to secure a new identify, which he used to stalk Sylvia all over again.

I still don't know how he found out she needed medical help for her persistent insomnia but once he knew she was in Valhalla he faked his own mental illness so as to be admitted. Apparently all he had to do was wander around Valhalla city stark naked with no ID. Doctors said he spit out all his medication and spit at the nurses as well. And so they just labeled him as non-compliant and kept him there. Then one night he cornered a visiting psychiatrist and beat the living hell out of him, leaving him for dead in the janitor's closet. He then put on the doctor's garb. Knowing he had limited time to make his move, he then approached Dr. Katz claiming to be the newly arrived resident Dr. Ashbury, who he'd left for dead in the janitor's closet. Posing as Dr. Ashbury, he then convinced Dr. Katz that Sylvia had a condition called "thought insertion" and that he too would like to have some input in her treatment. Then when he arrived in the office he asked for time alone with her and that is when it all went down.

I honestly don't know how it is after all she has been through that she is holding up so well. She is in amazing spirits and you can bet your ass she is getting her sleep.

Each day she gets a little better. She is not on any meds. In fact she has gone vegan and says she is purifying her mind, body, and soul.

CHAPTER FIFTY

SYLVIA

Hank is in bed watching the news with the sound off, while working on his laptop. As soon as he sees that I am awake he puts the laptop on the nightstand and turns to me and says, "Good afternoon, sleepy-head."

"Is it really? I guess I needed my beauty sleep."

"High-noon. And you were beautiful even when you weren't sleeping."

"Thank God those days are over."

"Yes, its all over now Baby Blue."

"Dylan?"

"Yup, gotta love some Bobby."

"That is a wonderful song. So evocative."

"What do you want to do today?" Hank asks.

"I don't know. I was kind of thinking that maybe, since we haven't done *it* for a while that we could, you know?"

"Do what?" he says, even though he knows damn well what I mean. I am already aroused by the thought of *it*.

"You know, mess around."

"You mean fuck around?" he says.

"If you must be so blunt."

He gently pulls me out of bed, I am topless in my

bright orange panties. He is dressed in his black satin boxers and the flip-flops that he often wears when he is working from home, like today. There is a floor-to-ceiling window in his master bedroom. Usually the oh-so-masculine dark grey curtains are down, as we treasure out privacy.

"Alexa," Hank says cordially, as if she were hired help, "open sesame."

He has programed those words to trigger the curtains opening. The curtains slowly lift, like we are in a Broadway theatre performance. Through the wall-sized window I can see that the day is overcast. Yet a ray of sun shoots through a break in the clouds like a spotlight which beams right into the bedroom. Across the way is the hustle and bustle of Union Square, and today the farmers market is in full swing. We are three flights up yet if a pedestrian New Yorker or a visiting tourist would look up they could see us through the window. I dare not check to see if anybody down there is craning their neck to look up and see me standing topless with my man.

Hank walks towards me and says, "You are a goddess." And then he lowers himself to kneel upon the floor on one knee. "And I would like to have the privilege of making you my wife."

I catch my breath for a moment.

He pulls off my panties, bringing them down to my knees. I am too stunned and turned on to reply. I lift each leg so that he can take my panties all the way off. Then he mimics what he might do as my groom and they were my garter belt and he opens the window, allowing the warm summer breeze to enter the room, and tosses them out of the window.

"It's absolutely breathtaking."

I think for a moment of all I have been through to arrive at this moment. And suddenly I can see a future for us. And it looks good to me. I pause for a moment knowing no matter my answer, knowing Hank, he will still proceed to make love to me. But I want to be made love to as his future wife. So I catch my breath and then say, "Absolutely, yes."

He bends to kiss my inner thighs, takes my hand and slips a diamond ring onto my finger, which sparkles in the light, and I totally forget that I am stark naked standing in front of a window facing the street.

He slips the engagement ring on my finger and then buries his face between my legs, progressing upwards with his kisses until he has a nipple in his mouth, while he probes me with his fingers.

He turns me to face the window, placing my hands on the glass so that I am slightly bent over, and plunges himself inside me, from behind.

I dare to look down and spot a man vending hot dogs. He has no customers. He just sits on a stool and stares up. Looking directly at me. He glances away for a moment but cannot stop himself from returning his gaze as Hank grinds into me. His groin pushing against my ass, his cock deep inside my pussy.

Nirvana is but a gasp away.

My body begins to shudder, and that is when I see a scraggly-looking guy with a skateboard turn his head towards the sky. He catches me rattling like an L train, cups a hand over his eyes like a hood to block out the sun and get a better look.

Hank fills me with his rock-hard powerful desire and I feel like everything is and everything will be alright.

CHAPTER FIFTY-ONE

Dear Sylvia,

What is real and what is not real is a matter of perspective. What is one person's truth is another's fallacy. And with that being said, I feel I ought to write you. Because I care about you. My intentions have always been noble even if my methods have not exactly been on the level. What does it matter now? I am locked up in a level five maximum security hospital for the criminally insane. So you should have no more worries about the likes of me. They do allow me to write with this old-fashioned Smith Corona typewriter. Thus, this letter to you.

I know that I breached our relationship. And I am sorry about the way things worked out. I never wished for you to doubt your thoughts. And many frail-minded individuals are perfectly content with their madness. They revel in it.

Let me just plant a seed of thought within you. Remember when I suggested you suffered from thought insertion disorder? Just let me insert this thought in you like your husband Hank inserts his penis into you. If you are still reading on.

Sylvia, what if everyone in your life were simply condescending to you? What if Hank just enjoyed his slice of paradise and his little piece of ass so much that he accepted living with a woman who does not have a grip on her own reality? Many elders live with loved ones falling into dementia and they keep on loving them anyway. They make love to them even though the recipient of their carnality may not even know who they are. A kind of rape really, if you ask me.

And so I present to you the possibility that your life simply isn't what it seems to be. Maybe people love you so much that they are afraid to just come out and tell you that you are a raving lunatic. Maybe your long-suffering father loves you so much that he allows you to believe in entire swatches of your life that simply are not factual.

Sylvia, you are so far gone that I tell you now that the woman you think you are is simply not real at all. Maybe once upon a time you were a little girl dreaming of becoming a princess and being saved by the prince. And in many ways you have been. As you now live in a castle in New York City where everyone that knows you keeps an eye on you to make sure you don't simply wander off and get lost in the oblivion of your fantasy.

And oh, your dearly departed mother, Anne. I know she must haunt you, her death so tragic.

And then there was Will, your second husband, who you shot down in cold blood because you got it into your head that he wanted you dead.

These are the fairytales you tell yourself.

Just like the tall tale you tell to anyone who'll listen about Scott, your rough around the edges roofer. A good guy. A meat and potatoes Midwest guy who you tarred with the label of a domestic abuser by claiming he'd hit you.

And who flies to your rescue in his private jet? Hank, of course. The man who at first wished to market your plight until it became too bloody even for the tabloids at the supermarket.

I guess you wished I had died on the floor of Valhalla at the hands of that beefy nurse. But I made it through. Sharks like me don't die easily. Now you have it in your mind that I had my lower jaw removed in order to fake my own death on the highway so that I could be the madman imposter psychiatrist at the very mental ward where you were stationed. And why?

It is all because I have followed your news story from the start. I had that black Porsche park in front of your house. I befriended your father and planted in him the inkling of an idea that you should seek psychotherapy. All because I have a fascination for fascinating women. Yes, there was one before you. But she did not work out for me. But then came you. And you must know that when I was a boy my mother committed me. Because I almost killed a boy who was bullying me. It was a ghastly incarceration that shattered me for life. The psychiatric community, I believed, attempted to control my mind. So I vowed the only way to beat 'em was to join 'em. So I became a physiatrist with the sole intention of doing unto others as they did unto me.

I saw something of myself in you. A certain homicidal sprit. Like I had when I was a boy. Before they snuffed that out of me. And my dream has always been to find, isolate and penetrate the psyche of someone who had tasted death. Like you tasted death when you shot your husband. I wanted to have you all to myself, to feel what you feel, to know what you know. To fuck with and to fuck your mind Sylvia, my Sylvia. Call it a platonic, satanic lust to sip the blood of a killer. But I have to accept that I was foiled once again.

You don't have to worry that I might be circling you like a shark anymore, because I can't. I have been locked up without a release date.

Yours eternally,
Dr. Meadows.

CHAPTER FIFTY-TWO

HANK

I hold this letter in my hands. It was taped with duck tape to my mailbox in the lobby of my building. The letter was in an unsealed envelope. It wasn't even addressed to anyone. I figured it was a note from the super or something to that effect. So I opened it. I am thankful that I have. There are all sorts of things I can do with this letter. And there is much to be done. I need to know how this got to my building. How Dr. Meadows knows where I live, as my address has never been listed. I might call the authorities and see if it is a fake. Maybe some troll who read about Sylvia's story online was trying to fuck with her head. Or just maybe it is real. What concerns me most is that somebody was able to pass the front desk to post it.

If this scumbag is incarcerated how could he make such arrangements to have this brought to the building where Sylvia and I live? Or maybe Dr. Meadows isn't locked up at all. Has he somehow escaped? Naw, that would only happen in a horror film. It is too incomprehensible to even fathom.

I tuck the letter into my jacket and take the elevator to my floor and imagine what it might be like to be locked up for the rest of my life.

Leaving the elevator I walk down the hall to my loft. *Our* loft now. As I ride the elevator, I think about the words I have read. And it calls to light something I have observed about Sylvia as of late when she sleeps. She has become one to sleep-talk. Mostly, she mumbles something that I never made any sense of until just now. One night she mumbled, "I am Anne," On another night, "I am Will." On another, "I am Scott." And one night she said she was me. Then I was shocked when she said, "I am Dr. Meadows." And now I see that we all live inside her. We are the voices both good and evil that live in her dreams. And in some ways it is all true. We are all living in Sylvia's mind.

In Sylvia's dream, I reach for the door and unlock it. That is when I make my decision.

Sylvia is inside with Sweetie at her bare feet, looking through fashion magazines and drinking fresh coffee.

"Oh, hi," she says, smiling.

I give her a hug that lasts longer than usual.

"My, aren't we feeling loving today. What's the occasion?" she asks.

"Do I need a reason to hug my wife?"

"I suppose not."

"Is there any more coffee?" I ask.

"Hey, make your own damn coffee," she jokes.

"Of course, you're a liberated woman."

"You're damn right I am," she says. "If anything, you can fucking serve me."

"Sounds fun," I say.

I put on a kettle of water with the plan to make coffee with our French Press. I have to think very hard as to where to hide this letter so that Sylvia can never, ever find it. I decide to put on some toast and purposely set the toaster on high to burn it.

I turn on a burner on the stove and hold the letter over the fire.

"Hey, what's that smell?" she asks.

"Don't worry, just some burned bread," I say, before the kitchen fire alarm goes off.

It's unbearably loud. By the time Sylvia enters the kitchen the paper has turned to ashes.

"What the hell have you burned?" she says.

I switch off the fire alarm, take Sylvia into my arms and say, "Just a little accident with my toast. I took care of it. Don't you worry your pretty little self about it any more."

ACKNOWLEDGEMENTS

Special thanks to the Dark Edge Press team — Leanne Braithwaite for your keen editorial eye, Louise Mullins for your generous spirit and Michael Norman for your literary prowess.

Ivan Jenson is a fine artist, novelist and popular contemporary poet. His artwork has featured in *Art in America*, *Art News*, and *Interview Magazine* and has sold at auction at Christie's. He was commissioned to paint the final portrait of the late Malcolm Forbes. And some of his work, commissioned by Absolut Vodka, has appeared in the Spritmuseum (yes it is spelled like that) in Stockholm, Sweden.

Art features a lot in Ivan's writing too. The novels, *Dead Artist* and *Seeing Soriah* illustrate the creative and often dramatic lives of artists. Jenson's poetry has been widely published throughout the globe, in a variety of literary media. He has also written three other novels titled: *Marketing Mia*, *Erotic Rights* and *The Murderess*.

Love crime fiction as much as we do?

Sign up to our associates program to be first in line to receive Advance Review Copies of our books, and to win stationary and signed, dedicated editions of our titles during our monthly competitions. Further details on our website: www.darkedgepress.co.uk

Follow @darkedgepress on Facebook, Twitter, and Instagram to stay updated on our latest releases.

Printed in Great Britain
by Amazon